Winner books are produced by Victor Books and are designed to entertain and instruct young readers in Christian principles. Each book has been approved by specialists in Christian education and children's literature. These books uphold the teachings and principles of the Bible.

Other Winner Books you will enjoy:

Sarah and the Magic Twenty-fifth, by Margaret Epp

Sarah and the Pelican, by Margaret Epp

The Hairy Brown Angel and Other Animal Tails, edited by Grace Fox

Danger on the Alaskan Trail (three stories)

Gopher Hole Treasure Hunt, by Ralph Bartholomew

Daddy, Come Home, by Irene Aiken

Patches, by Edith V. Buck

BATTLE
AT THE
BLUE LINE

P. C. Fredricks

illustrations by
Ken Shields

A WINNER BOOK

VICTOR BOOKS

a division of SP Publications, Inc., Wheaton, Illinois
Offices also in Fullerton, California • Whitby, Ontario, Canada • London, England

Scripture is from the King James Version unless indicated otherwise. Other quotations are from *The New International Version:* New Testament, © 1973, The New York Bible Society International. Used by permission.

Library of Congress Catalog Card No. 77-090327
ISBN: 0-88207-482-2

VICTOR BOOKS
A division of SP Publications, Inc.
P. O. Box 1825 • Wheaton, Ill. 60187

CONTENTS

Preface

The persons and events in *Battle at the Blue Line* have grown out of the thousands of fragmented memories of a hockey parent who has driven sons and their friends to hundreds of games:

The snow-blown roads,

Sweat-scented dressing rooms,

Frost-fringed arena bleachers.

The glitter of the red- and blue-lined ice surface.

The clang of skates, the slap of sticks, and the crash of young bodies.

The breathless groan when a boy goes down—and is still.

The quick cheer when he stirs—and gets up unhurt.

The thunder of a standing cheer ringing in steel rafters.

And the glow in a boy's eyes when he knows he's worked his hardest and bettered his best performance.

For all such hockey heroes, and especially for my son who clued me in, thanks from a hockey parent.

ICE HOCKEY FLOOR PLAN

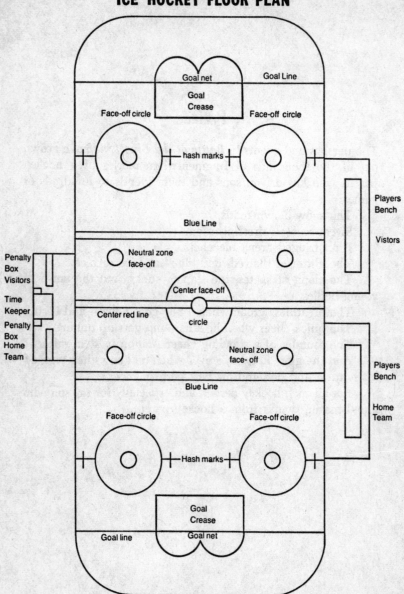

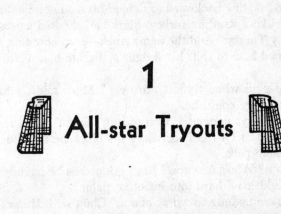

1
All-star Tryouts

"Hey, Mark, I can't believe we're really here!" Brad Phillips turned and scanned the dressing room from its overhead, wire-caged lights to the rubber matting on the damp concrete floor.

Around the circle of benches, boys struggled into their uniforms, some only in their long underwear worn under hockey equipment. Others were already fully dressed in the Oak River uniform, helmeted, gloved, and with their skates laced.

"It's our big day, Turkey!" Brad's red-haired, freckled friend commented. "The day we've had circled on the calendar since the all-star [1] tryouts were posted back in September."

Brad and Mark began to get into their gear. Both had trouble wiggling into the snug red-and-white hockey shirts. Ever since they'd taken part in their first team sport in kindergarten some eight years before, they'd had trouble fitting into uniforms the team gave them.

It was Mark who had slapped the label "Turkey" on Brad when they played their first hockey game. Brad had been

---

[1] An *all-star* team is chosen from the best players in one age group from the various communities covered by an arena—to represent that arena in tournaments.

caught in a two-on-one breakaway.[2] His beginner's waddle, as he tried skating backward to defend his own net, had made him look like a strutting turkey. Mark had shouted across the rink, "Hey Turkey!" And the name stuck—even now that Brad had learned how to shift his weight and skate backward with ease.

"I'll be glad when tryouts are over," Mark said. "I forgot how scary they could be!"

"Are you guys nervous?" Tom (Chug) Evans asked. He lay on his stomach on the floor while his older brother buckled on his goalie pads.

"Nervous? Who's nervous?" Brad grinned as he pounded his gloved right hand hard into his other palm.

"You have nothing to worry about," Chug said. He grunted as his brother yanked a chest buckle tighter.

That's all right for you to say, thought Brad. *Your Dad's the coach. The team will carry two goalies, and there are only three trying out. That gives you a two out of three chance.*

But for a defenseman? Brad glanced around. There must be 30 guys there. And probably another 30 in dressing room #2. And they were still coming. Eighty guys could be trying out for the 17 places on the all-star team. He didn't even know all the fellows he'd be competing against.

Oh, sure, he knew the Oak River kids. He'd played with them before and knew that none were a threat to his position. Jerry Maloney was a centerman. Flip Sawyer was a left-winger, and Mike Rawleigh a right-winger. Mark played right defense while Brad played left.

Brad eyed the other fellows critically. He'd seen some of them on the school bus. He knew their first names. Pete, a small kid, had moved into the Old Holbrook homestead last summer.

---

[2] *Breakaway* occurs when a player gets the puck away from an opponent, skates past the last defender, and has a clear shot on the goal.

Kurt, a kid with a British accent and private school manners, lived in a big, new house built on Acorn Creek. Neither Pete nor Kurt were as tough as the good local hockey players. But they had expensive equipment and could be all-city talent.

"Crumb!" Mark shattered Brad's thoughtful silence. "The nervous look on your face is giving me jitters. We have nothing to get excited about. We've been on all-star teams before and we will be again."

Sure, Brad thought. *Your dad's Joe LaBlanc, the all-star team manager! And my dad's—*

Suddenly, 13-year-old Brad felt very alone—almost scared. His dad was dead. Killed in a construction accident, six years ago. He didn't think about his dad much anymore—except at times like this, when he was scared.

His mother often reminded him that he had a father, the heavenly Father spelled with a capital F. The Father and Friend who sticks closer than a brother (Prov. 18:24).

"C'mon, Turkey," Mark opened the dressing room door and Brad followed.

Once out on the fresh ice surface in the Oak River Arena, Brad circled in long, easy strides to stretch his muscles for the ordeal ahead.

Whistles blew and the team assembled for drills: stopping and starting, forward and backward. Drills for passing, shooting, deflecting, and rebounding. Each player reached for greater agility and more speed.

Soon, in the heat of his all-out effort, Brad forgot about the strapped-on plastic number that identified him on the clipboards held by the three coaches. He forgot everything except the feeling of flying on blades.

A whistle shrilled and Coach Evans let out a bellow that brought the 89 guys to attention on the ice, fatigue forgotten. "This is a double practice!" he told them. "Skill without stamina is no good in tournament hockey. This is a double tryout!" The electric digits blinked on—30 minutes to go.

Brad's tanned face sagged into a sweaty grin. His brown eyes snapped with determination as he led the pack into new fast-skating circles. He'd exercised, worked, and even prayed for this chance. He felt fatigue, but he didn't intend to show it if he could help it.

Brad obeyed the whistles and commands with one part of himself, leaving another part free to delight in what he was doing. His blades barely cut ice, and he felt as if he were skating on air. It was just Brad Phillips, a game he loved, and a Friend. He saw only the white ice ahead of him. Heard only the slush-shush of his own skate blades and the coach's whistle.

It was only after the last long blast of the whistle that Brad felt his soggy pads clinging to him and realized that his knees felt like rubber.

Coach Evans and Tom Maloney stood on either side of the gate that led from the ice to three locker rooms, and called out a room number to each boy as he left the ice.

"Phillips, room 3."

Three! Was he scrapped in the first cut? After last year's tryouts, room 3 was the "cuts." Room 2 was the "possibles" and room 1 the players who'd made the all-star team.

Brad couldn't believe it. Was he cut already? No, it couldn't be. But it could! Just because he'd been on the same team as Chug, Mark, and Jerry didn't necessarily mean that he was automatically on the all-star team.

Now Brad felt the sting of sweat trickling down his forehead and into his eyes. He sank onto the bench in room 3, seeing nothing through the damp towel that he draped over his head.

He'd given the tryouts all the skill and speed he had. He'd skated, stickhandled, and drilled with complete concentration. The choice of all-star team members wasn't his. But the butterflies in his empty stomach certainly were.

He pulled the towel off his head and saw Mark sitting next to him. His friend's freckled face was frozen into a frown. Chug was there too. His square jaw set as he paced in front of them. Brad knew then that even these guys thought they hadn't made the all-star team.

The dressing room door opened and Coach Evans walked in, clipboard in hand. He looked around the room at the troubled faces and grinned. "You fellows weren't culled out of the crowd to go to jail! You're the new Oak River Otters all-star team!"

After a few seconds of stunned silence, the whole room exploded like all the fireworks at the Canadian National Exhibition and the Fourth of July going off at once. Gloves and shirts flew as boys pounded each other and shouted, "Dyn-O-mite! Decent! Wow!"

"Hey, Turkey, we made it!" Mark yelled as he slapped Brad's hands. "Maybe we'll get to play against my cousin Steve, on the Beaver Bridge all-stars. We made it, Turkey. We made it!"

Joe LaBlanc, Mark's dad, began handing out player permission cards. "That nickname, Turkey, doesn't fit anymore," he said, smiling. "Not the way Brad skated today!"

Suddenly Brad felt 10 feet tall—as if Mr. LaBlanc had just hung an Olympic gold medal on him.

Now everybody scrambled to get out of soggy equipment and into jeans, to spread the good news.

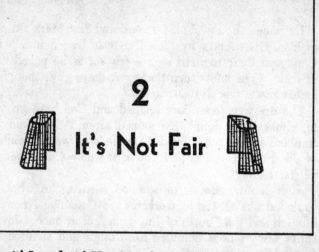

2
It's Not Fair

"I made it! I made it! Hey Mom? I made it!" In one burst of energy Brad Phillips managed to drop his loaded hockey bag, slam the kitchen door, throw his hat into the air, and shout, "Dyn-O-mite! I made it, Mom. I made it!"

Mrs. Phillips closed the oven door and turned to see what her youngest son had done now.

Brad shed a snowy sports jacket, peeled off a red, sweat-streaked hockey shirt, and dumped snow-coated boots on the drip mat before opening his bag.

Mrs. Phillips picked up Brad's red sweater and held it up. "I hope you weren't inside when this happened." She pointed to a big boot mark in the middle of the back.

"Sorry about that, Mom. Dressing room 3 went wild when Coach Evans said the last cuts were in rooms 1 and 2. We made it!"

Gary, Brad's older brother, said, "Don't blame the dressing room. It was that pack of hockey hoodlums that went wild."

"Should I ask *what* you made?" his mother asked.

"This!" Brad jerked a new, red helmet complete with face cage and number 4 from his bag. "Rink issue for our Oak

River Bantam [3] entry into the Georgian Valley Tournament."

Brad let out a long whistle of satisfaction. "Mom, this is the most exciting thing that's ever happened to me!"

Gary snorted in disgust. "That's what you said last week when you won a pizza at that store opening in the Georgian Plaza."

Brad glanced quickly from his brother to his mother. He hadn't expected them to be as excited about this as he was, but he thought they'd at least show some interest.

"Look, Mom," Brad rapped his knuckles against the industrial strength helmet. "It's free—mine to wear for the Oak River Otters—"

"Oh brother!" Gary interrupted. "Wouldn't you know it? Free!" Gary tucked his expensive crutches under his arms and stumped angrily around Brad's hockey equipment on the kitchen floor.

"Yeah! All the guys who made the team . . ." Brad knew he spoke the words quietly, but they exploded against his eardrums. He noticed his mother's eyes sadden as she watched Gary staring at snow swirling beyond the living room window.

All the heart-pounding excitement he'd felt just a few minutes before, suddenly died and dropped heavily to the pit of his stomach. He knew his mother wouldn't hear a word he said when she looked at Gary that way. When she worried about Gary, she seemed to pull a soundproof helmet over her head.

But making the tournament team meant too much to Brad not to try to get her attention. "Mom, Mom, 89 boys tried out for the team. Only 17 made it. I'm one of that 17!"

"That's nice," Mrs. Phillips said automatically. Then she blinked as if coming out of a dream. "I'm sorry, Brad, I didn't hear what you said. I was thinking of something else."

---

[3] *Bantam* is the name given to hockey players 13-14 years of age in Canada's Ontario Minor Hockey Association league called the House League.

Brad repeated what he'd just said. And from the look on his mother's face, he knew that she wanted to say, "With 88 others to choose from, why did they have to pick you?"

But she didn't. Mom was too kind to say that—especially in his moment of triumph.

Suddenly all the fatigue Brad hadn't felt during tryouts hit his muscles like a slap shot in the ribs.

He heaved a big sigh and slowly headed for the basement clothesline with a bundle of hockey pads and equipment piled in his arms. The excitement of making the team must have blown his mind. He'd forgotten all about his brother's handicap.

He'd even forgotten he had a brother and about Mom working in the craft shop with Aunt Kate.

Out on the fresh ice surface, he'd been unaware of anything except that secure feeling of accomplishment and having a Friend beside him.

I could sure use a friend now! Brad told himself. His mom had her eyes on Gary. His dad—

Brad hung his soggy hockey pads, pants, socks, and sweater on the clothesline in the furnace room, and painfully climbed the stairs to the shower.

He hadn't meant to cause trouble. But he had forgotten his brother's appointments at the hospital in Toronto. Brad's making the team would mean more driving for Mom. One more thing for her to do.

But making the all-star team was such an important thing to a 13-year-old. He would be part of the first all-star team to represent the new arena. A happening! A beautiful, beautiful happening!

At least it had been until he saw the look on his mother's face.

How could anything that he'd tried so hard for, and won, suddenly blow up in his face?

He set the water temperature and stepped under the hot spray of the shower.

"Ooooh!" Brad winced as he lathered the large bruise on his shoulder. No one had checked [4] him that hard, had they?

Of course not! He grinned as he remembered Mark pounding his shoulder when they heard they were on the team.

Brad sighed as he towelled his hair, then pulled on clean jeans and a T-shirt. How could he be so dumb—get so carried away? This wouldn't be his usual Oak River Otters team, playing a game away and getting back within a couple of hours.

Tournament games were often played so far from home that players were responsible for their own transportation.

Life just wasn't fair, at least not to a guy with a handicapped brother—and no dad.

Sometimes Brad wondered *who* was the real accident victim. People would say to him, "I'd think you'd be grateful it wasn't you, and be willing to make allowances for your poor brother . . ."

And it seemed as if all he did was make allowances—try to be thoughtful, try to forgive Gary's sarcasm. Instead of playing soccer last summer, he made trips to the hospital with Gary and Mom each week, lifting the wheelchair in and out of the station wagon, waiting in hospital waiting rooms. It was no fun breathing in hospital smells when his friends were out enjoying the fresh air!

It had been rough after Dad died. But Brad had Gary to depend on. They did things together. They swam in the river in summer, skated on the pond in winter.

Then last spring a sleepy driver swerved to miss a dog and hit Gary who was delivering early morning newspapers on his

---

[4] *Checking*: The body check is the use of one's body to slow down or stop the progress of an opponent. It requires a lot of physical skill to do it without incurring a penalty.

bicycle. After the accident it was *Brad* doing things for *Gary.*

But Gary wasn't in a wheelchair anymore. He was fitted with braces and though he still couldn't move his legs, he was able to get around with crutches.

But I'm not handicapped! Brad argued with himself. *So I won't drop the all-star hockey tournament. Not even if Mom is praying that I will!*

Brad grabbed a sponge, wiped the tub, dropped his sweaty clothes into the hamper and headed toward the kitchen where dinner was waiting.

Gary dropped his crutches where Brad had to step over them to get to his place at the back of the table. Mrs. Phillips noticed but pretended she didn't. She'd pulled an invisible mask over her soundproof helmet. A smile on that mask warned, "God's in His heaven; all's right with the world," and she wouldn't see anything that said otherwise.

Suddenly Brad wasn't hungry anymore.

Mother looked up from 'grace,' smiling brightly as she said, "I had Mike Rawleigh's dad check the station wagon today. He says it could go another 70,000 miles." She sighed. "It had me worried, especially with the trip to Toronto tomorrow."

Brad knew it was no use to say anything about the team now. Mealtime was family time—without hassles.

The first practice was the day after tomorrow, less than 48 hours away. "Be on time! Be fully equipped!" Coach Evans had bellowed the words at the successful boys. "Be on the ice by 7 P.M.!"

That meant the player card had to be completed—and signed by a parent—*before* ice time.

Brad ate his supper, but his stomach was churning so much that it didn't know whether he had eaten his dinner or sawdust.

Brad knew that many other boys waited eagerly to jump into the spot he'd earned on that team. And it wouldn't even help if he ran away from home. He had to have a parent's signature on that card. And Mom was his only parent.

"I want you to help me with the dishes tonight, Brad," Mom said.

"Why does it always have to be me?" Brad groaned. "Gary's hands aren't handicapped. He doesn't do dishes with his feet."

"What an awful thing to say, Brad," his mother scolded. "You know Gary is in pain."

Brad looked at his brother, slouched in a reclining chair, reading the paper. He didn't look as if he had pain.

Silently, Brad started stacking dishes.

If I were a cripple, Mom would care, Brad told himself. *She'd be asking questions like, "How's everything today? How do you feel? Anything I can do to help?"*

"Mom, it's not fair!" The words were out before Brad knew what he was saying. "Why should one handicapped person make the whole family feel handicapped?"

His mother gasped. "That's not a nice accusation."

"It's not a nice spot to be in," Brad said, "not when I've made the all-star team!"

"You're really uptight about this team," his mother commented.

"Why shouldn't I be? I've got two good legs. I can skate. I made the team. Why shouldn't I play hockey? *Because Gary can't?*"

Brad's voice quavered, but having said that much, he knew he might as well say it all. So he rushed on. "It's just not fair. I know all about the 'making allowances' bit. I didn't play soccer last summer or even swim much. I know you don't go to as many things as you used to at church and you work longer hours.

"But, Mom, if I have to give up my chance to play all-star hockey, I want a good reason!"

The only sounds in the kitchen after Brad's outburst were

the swishing of soapy water and the click of dinner plates. And his mother's breathing—as if she were running.

Brad waited.

When Mrs. Phillips looked up from her work her face was red and her eyes were filled with tears.

"Mom, I—" Brad stopped short. He hadn't meant to hurt her.

"Brad," his mother said slowly, "an intelligent boy deserves a reason for a decision concerning him. I—I just don't know what to say—"

"Mom," Brad interrupted, "I've prayed for this. I've worked out. I've made the team. Other fathers and mothers were cheering and congratulating their kids. I felt 10 feet tall! I came roaring home to tell you . . . and suddenly it was all wrong!

"If Gary walks to the mailbox on crutches without falling, it's a big deal! Yet every normal, healthy thing I do is a big problem. It's just not fair!"

Brad clattered around as he dried the plates.

"What's a guy supposed to do?" he continued. "If I'm a winner at the arena, I'm a loser at home. If I'm a winner at school, I'm a loser at church. Like the time my math project was in the newspaper and my Sunday School teacher warned me, 'pride goeth before a fall.' What's a guy supposed to do?"

Mom rinsed out the sink and picked up a towel to help Brad dry dishes, for Brad's mind was working harder on his problem than his hands were.

"Mom," Brad continued, "trying out for the team was really great—praying about something and then doing it better than I'd ever hoped possible. But when I got home, *it was all wrong!* How can something be so right for me out there, and so wrong for me here at home? It's the same me!"

"Brad," his mother began, "you have the problem we all have with the many different roles we must play. You're a student at school, a worshiper in church, a teammate at the arena, and a brother and a son at home. Sometimes the different roles clash with each other. Sometimes there's just not enough of one person to cover all the roles."

It was his mother who sighed this time. "In a sense, Brad, one handicapped person in a family does handicap the family because it adds to our responsibilities. Since Gary's accident—"

This was the first time she'd ever talked to Brad as if he were an adult.

"No matter how difficult the roles one person must fill, if we feel right about them and are honest with God, as well as with ourselves, they will work out OK. Maybe not the way we expect or the way we want, but right for us. Can you understand that, Brad?"

Brad nodded.

"Congratulations, Son. I'm glad you tried and won—even though your making the team does add one more thing to the family schedule." She put a hand on Brad's bruised shoulder, and he tried not to wince.

"Leave your game schedule by the phone. I'll see if I can trade some work hours with Aunt Kate so I can be free for your games."

"I'll try and round up rides with the guys too. Thanks, Mom. Thanks a lot!" Brad breathed a little easier.

That Friend that sticks closer than a brother—that Friend who skated with him *was still with him.* Brad unfolded a crumpled game schedule he'd put in his hip pocket earlier and wrote on it "players must be in the dressing room one half hour before the game times listed." Then he pinned the schedule to the bulletin board in the kitchen.

He still didn't know if he was a winner or a loser in today's "tryouts" at home. But at least he didn't feel like a loser anymore.

His mom had listened. She'd even talked eyeball-to-eyeball

with him. And he'd do all he could to be sure his attitudes were right.

That night Brad thumbed through his Bible before he went to sleep. He turned to his favorite passage in the Gospel of Matthew. As he read those paragraphs, certain verses stood out in his mind: "Your Father knows what you need before you ask Him," and "For if you forgive men when they sin against you, your heavenly Father will also forgive you" (Matthew 6:8, 14, NIV).

Thank You, Father, Brad prayed. *Thank You for knowing what I need before I ask.*

Forgive me for feeling angry with people and all their advice and for feeling cheated and resentful. I've spent almost all my time helping Gary, and I feel cheated out of swimming and soccer. Now I'm afraid of being cheated out of all-star hockey.

I didn't mean to get mad at Mom tonight, Father. And I don't want to make more work for her. I want to play tournament hockey.

Help me to accept not being able to play in this year's tournament, if it's not Your will that I play.

I love You, Father.

Then Brad sat up in his bed and thought about the day's events.

The tryouts had been great. His Friend had helped Brad make a dream come true. So where did that ugly, empty feeling inside come from? He didn't have it as he walked home the four blocks from the arena. Not even when Mom spotted the boot mark on his sweater.

So where? When? What had caused him to feel this way?

Then Brad remembered! Gary had snapped, "That's what you said last week when you won that pizza." That's when the ugly feeling developed. Brad also remembered how Gary had glowered at the red helmet—as if he'd like to stomp it to bits under his crutches.

So it was resentment—and anger toward Gary because Gary seemed to stand between him and his mom, between him and hockey!

Help me get rid of this awful feeling, Father, he prayed. *Forgive me for the anger, the resentment.*

The phone range—once, twice. Brad heard it clearly through the air vent from the kitchen below.

His mother answered. Her voice quickened as she explained to Aunt Kate about Brad wanting to play all-star hockey. "Some of the practices conflict with Gary's hospital appointments," she said, "but the actual games will be played Christmas week."

Brad let out a long sigh, lay back on his bed, and stared at the ceiling. He wasn't sure he could find rides to all the tournament games. But whatever, he vowed he wouldn't blame Gary again. Gary couldn't help it if he needed therapy 100 miles south, when Brad needed to practice hockey 60 miles east.

3
Doctor's Advice

Brad woke up to a gray November morning. Immediately he remembered that he still needed his mother's permission to play hockey—also rides to the Beaver Bridge arena during tournament week. But the tension and emptiness he had felt the night before were gone.

Then he remembered that Gary had a medical appointment that day, and groaned. The last one turned into a six-hour ordeal with Gary being fitted with braces and all.

If Brad could arrange rides with other parents and not expect Mom to drive, then maybe she'd sign the player card in spite of these trips to the hospital.

He rushed downstairs, hoping that the doctor would give Gary a clean bill of health this time. Maybe there'd be no more therapy or fittings or braces—at least until Gary had grown more. Gary wasn't actually sick. He ate, slept, and functioned like anybody else, except that he needed crutches to get around.

"Brad! You're not going to wear those frightful jeans!" his mother exclaimed when she saw him.

Brad scanned his frayed, patched, but favorite jeans.

"They're clean," he said. "I always wear them to school, except when you wash them."

"But you're not going to school. This appointment is for the *family*."

"You mean I can't go to school today at all?" Brad asked. If he couldn't see the guys, he wouldn't be able to round up rides with their parents!

Just then Gary stomped out of the washroom. "Since when has school been so big with you?"

"Brad, I told you—" Mom said.

"I forgot, Mom." Brad wondered if this was going to be the kind of day where one thing after another hit a guy like a frozen hockey puck in the stomach.

"You forget everything except hockey," Gary accused.

Brad turned away from his brother's scowl and sat down at the table. Breakfast was unusually quiet since they were in a hurry to get on their way.

On the 100-mile drive to the clinic in Toronto, Gary sat in the back of the station wagon with his legs stretched across the seat. Brad couldn't see him but he could hear him—loud and clear.

"The news media will cover the tournament. The TV station will take film clips for the sportscasts," Gary said. "You know how some church members frown on sports—paying entrance fees to sporting events and playing games on Sunday."

Brad didn't feel like arguing today, so only the whine of the snowtires on the freeway broke the silence in the car for a while.

Finally Mrs. Phillips spoke up. "Brad, can I talk straight to you?" she said.

"Is there any other way?" Brad answered, grinning. But his stomach muscles tightened as if he were expecting another slap shot in the stomach.

"It's only fair that you be given your chance to play in this tournament," his mother said. "But I just don't want to be a hockey mother!"

Gary choked back laughter with a cough. "And get thrown out of the arena for swearing at the referees like Katie Maloney?"

Brad swung around to deny the possibility of their mother ever cursing and saw the "I caught you this time" smirk on his brother's face.

Again, he let Gary's remark pass, but turned to his mother. "Aw, Mom, you don't need to worry about getting so involved in the game that you become a hockey mother. Not all the mothers with sons who play hockey end up cussing the referees."

"Katie Maloney does have a big mouth," Gary admitted.

Mom finally nodded. "I guess you're right. Hockey doesn't make good people bad or bad ones good. It just brings out what's already there."

Gary gave his "oh brother" groan.

"You know, Brad, I mentioned that this was a family appointment with Dr. Vanderberg," Mother said. "I'll ask him today about your playing hockey. His expert advice should help in a decision that affects the whole family."

Brad groaned silently. Dr. Vanderberg was Gary's doctor. Why should he care about *Brad* playing hockey?

High-rise buildings loomed around them as they came into Toronto. Brad didn't hold out much hope for making the team without a dad to vote for it. But he did have a heavenly Father. *Father*, he breathed, *Father, aren't You going to cast Your vote?*

Mom took the Dufferin Street ramp off highway 401 to the Yorkdale Mall where there were ground floor washrooms and a coffee bar—a place to freshen up before heading into downtown traffic to the hospital.

Gary made his usual bid to stay in the car. He didn't want

anything to eat or drink. He always avoided public places as much as possible—getting into church early and leaving late and baiting Mom into driving him to school so he wouldn't have to ride the school bus. Although he handled his crutches well, he sometimes stumbled over unfamiliar ground.

On the last stretch through city streets, the boys watched for "No Left Turn" signs and "One Way" streets that could make the therapy trip expensive.

Once safely parked near the hospital, Mrs. Phillips turned off the ignition and let out a long sigh.

Gary snorted. "Today's driving is a cinch to what the township roads will be like during the tournament."

Brad knew his brother meant it for another hockey putdown, but suddenly sensed something else: *Gary is afraid I'm winning! He's fighting all-star hockey for his own reasons. He's not fighting me!*

Dr. Vanderberg was a lean man, like the skiers who stopped at the Oak River General Store for weekend supplies.

After the usual few minutes of talk, he scanned several pages from a folder, making conversational sounds as he did so —"humph, hmmmm, very good. I see.

"You've had some bad turns these past few years, Mrs. Phillips. Are things straightening out for you now?"

Ruth Phillips let out a long sigh, as if she didn't know how to answer. "Some days I think so, but . . ."

"But every day can throw you new curves?" He nodded. I have two growing boys too. They're a few years older than yours, but I remember when they were 13 to 16 years old. He shuffled papers, then looked squarely at each of them in turn.

"Hundreds of families with handicapped children live normal active lives. It takes more planning and more determination on the part of everyone at first."

Brad braced himself for another hockey puck in the stomach.

"There is one thing," Mom began.

Brad heard Gary hiss air through clenched teeth. He heard his mother's anxious breathing. And he felt his own heart thumping.

The doctor leaned back in his chair and nodded as Ruth explained about Brad and the hockey tournament, her work schedule, Gary, and the driving.

"Hmmm. . . ." The doctor swung his chair to face Brad. "What position do you play?"

"Left defense, sir. I play right defense too, sometimes."

"Are you good?"

Brad grinned. "Yes, sir, most of the time."

Dr. Vanderberg nodded. "Why play hockey?"

"Why not hockey?" Brad replied quietly. "It's the greatest feeling in the world to play better than you've ever played before—and win!"

"Every person needs that, Brad." The doctor sounded very serious as he added, "Even adults like your mother need to get involved with something outside of themselves. And handicapped people like Gary. Tell me, Ruth, when was the last time you stood up and cheered for something?"

"I'm afraid I've been cheering silently these last few years," she said without looking up.

"Gary, when is the last time you yelled in any public place —the street, a playground, or an arena?" The doctor looked squarely at Gary.

"When that stupid fool missed a dog and hit me—over a year ago now."

"Your back was injured then, but your ability to yell wasn't."

"I think the idea of shouting in public is . . . is . . . *stupid!* Those healthy-as-a-horse hoodlums my brother runs around with act like a bunch of animals, fighting over a useless piece of black rubber like a pack of howling wolves!"

"Have you played hockey?" Dr. Vanderberg asked.

"House league," [5] Gary continued. "That was before this." He jerked his braces and a crutch clattered on the floor.

"I know how they pick the all-star teams. The coaches judge them for speed and strength by racing them around in circles, and by making them stop, start, and jump hurdles like a horse show. Maybe the coaches even look at their teeth to see how old they are!" Gary leaned back, his face was pale and muscle spasms made his right leg jerk uncontrollably.

Suddenly the doctor asked, "Ruth, what do you think of Brad playing in tournament hockey?"

"I enjoy watching the boys play. But with after-Christmas inventory at the shop, and Gary needing trips to the clinic, more driving seems out of the question."

"We're a skiing family," Doctor Vanderberg said after a minute of silence. "But our youngest son wanted to play hockey. At first I thought it a waste of time—a team of clods making a lot of noise about nothing, like you said, Gary. To make my son happy, I bought a hockey encyclopedia. When I learned why the spectators shouted, why the referees picked certain spots to drop the puck, and why they sent players to a penalty box,[6] I began to like the game a little better."

"Oh brother," Gary groaned.

"It was only my ignorance of the game that made me think it was a stupid sport. I grew to understand why it's such an exhausting game. It's even tiring for the spectators!"

Gary stared at his crutches as if he wished he could hide behind them.

"I strongly recommend that you resume your normal activities," he continued. "Gary is in good health. He can walk almost anywhere as long as he uses his crutches."

---

[5] *House league* is Canada's Ontario Minor Hockey Association League in which every child who registers is given a chance to play in his own age group regardless of experience or skill.

[6] *Penalty Box* is an area off the ice designated for players who must sit out parts of the game for breaking certain rules.

Brad felt a bubble of hope rising inside him.

The doctor looked at Gary again. "Let the kids on the school bus wait for you to enter and exit at *your* normal pace. It'll help keep you in the mainstream of life. Each person needs normal contacts with people his own age.

"And remember, crutches are no real handicap to being a hockey fan."

The doctor tipped his chair forward, made some notes in the folder, then spoke to each boy. He asked Brad several questions about hockey tournaments.

But to Gary he spoke as doctor to patient. "I know of no better place than a hockey arena for a person to shout, scream, and then go home without shame or guilt. The real handicapped person is the one who doesn't have such family activities. Even if you hate hockey, Gary, it's one way to start moving freely among nonhandicapped people."

He was speaking slowly now, "People will stare at you. But they will stare less if you're involved in the normal activities of the nonhandicapped."

Gary glowered at something on the doctor's desk, saying nothing.

"Tell me, Gary, what kind of braces did my secretary wear?"

Gary shifted his gaze. "None! I mean, I didn't see any."

"See what I mean?" Doctor Vanderberg said. "She wasn't acting like a handicapped person. Even though she wears a leg brace, she's busy earning her living, like any normal young lady. She's an excellent secretary too."

Finally the session was over and the rising bubble of hope burst inside Brad like thunder in his ears.

I made it! I made it! I finally made the team at home!

4

 Practice
and Prayer

From that great moment in the doctor's office, through the next five weeks, time turned like a lopsided wheel: clump, clump. It was the clump of Brad's red hockey bag hitting the kitchen floor some time after 8:30 every evening, six days a week.

Out on the ice with the team—skating, stickhandling, and taking shots on goal, that exciting lighter-than-air feeling filled him.

But once his bag hit the kitchen floor, Gary was there, ready to deflate him. "If I've got to go to that tournament, I've got to go," he grumbled. "But remember, dear brother, those fighting animals are *your* friends, not mine! Don't even let on that you know me, because I'm not going to let on I know you!"

And there was his mother who worried too much. "All the doctors have given us good advice since Gary's accident," she said. "We can only hope this is the same."

And Brad wondered over and over, *What if the team is put out in the first round? Boy, would Gary have the last laugh then!*

Each night at prayertime he said to himself, *That's the risk a guy takes. I asked the Father to help—and He did! So one team wins and one team loses. There are no tie games in tournament hockey; a tie goes into sudden death* [7] *overtime.*

This was one game the Otters had better win. And Brad was one Otter who'd give it all he had—practice and prayer.

"Hi Mom," Brad said when he got home from practice the next evening. He dropped onto the first chair inside the door. "This has got to be the sweetest tiredness a guy ever felt!"

"Well, it doesn't smell so sweet!" his mother said. "Get that stuff on the line before you shower."

Brad felt that if he moved a muscle it would zing in two like a worn-out rubberband. He opened his mouth to ask for time-out, but saw Gary and didn't.

"Remember, you asked for it!" Gary sneered, "So groan, brother, groan!" Then he pretended to trip over Brad's skates. "Sure glad something else besides me and my crutches is getting booted out of the way."

Brad shouldered his bag, grabbed his skates, and headed for the basement.

The miracle of making the team at home was still such a big, beautiful thing inside him, it seemed to light up everything that happened. Like now. Suddenly Brad knew that Gary was as resentful of him making the team, as Brad had been when he thought he wasn't going to make it because of Gary.

On his way to the shower, Brad caught a glimpse of his brother and noticed just how clumsy he looked on the crutches with his pivoting forearms and cuff-length cradle grip. Brad wanted to tell him about that Friend who'd been with him in the all-out test on the ice. And about the Father who'd helped him give up resentment in the battle to make the team at home. And about the sweet taste of victory *after* a guy starts getting it all straight inside.

---

[7] *Sudden death overtime* is the same as overtime play, except the first team to score, regardless of time, is declared the winner.

But how could he say something like that when Gary resented him so much? "Look Gary, He did it for me. Give up resentment and He'll straighten it all out for you too!" Saying it to a brother who would never again have the use of his legs would sound like so much superreligious talk—or boasting, he was sure.

So what could he do for his brother? Nothing?

Brad set the shower nozzle and felt the splashing warmth wash over him, felt his sore muscles loosen and his bruised shoulder ease.

Pray for Gary, that's what Brad could do.

And Gary wouldn't even know. He couldn't come out with any of his pet answers: "Don't give me any of that 'according to my faith' bit. Faith didn't get back my legs—even when I *did* believe. What good is faith?"

Yes, Brad could do for his brother just what he did for himself—talk to the Father.

So through late November and December Brad's days were set: School, hockey practice, shower, supper, chores, homework. Then Bible reading and sleep. He hardly noticed Gary now—except to watch him get on and off the school bus. And to pray for him at night.

Mom no longer drove Gary to and from the Oakland County Consolidated School. She was able to work full-time at the Shop now, getting home not long before Brad. Sometimes she brought home Christmas parcels and hid them as soon as she got them in the kitchen door. She often hummed as she planned meals for the next day.

One evening Aunt Kate visited the family. People said she looked like her brother, the boys' dad, with her hazel eyes, olive skin, and tall leanness.

"Hey, Aunt Kate?" Brad asked, "are you coming to our first tournament game? It's during Christmas vacation, on Dec. 26th."

"I'm trading work hours with your mom so she can be there," she said, gripping Brad's biceps. "You make it to the championship game, and I'll close up shop."

Mom passed a pan of fresh, hot cookies under their noses on her way from the oven to the counter. "I'm working till 9 o'clock tomorrow night, so you boys will be on your own for supper," she directed. "Heat that crock of maple-baked pork and beans—and have these cookies and applesauce."

Aunt Kate and Brad helped themselves to a warm, gumdrop cookie. "Umm good. Try one, Gary," Brad said, his mouth full. "You don't know what you're missing."

"The gumdrops stick to my teeth."

"So does peanut butter," Aunt Kate added. "But that never stopped you from eating it."

"Do I have to? Is what I eat part of this return to normal activities the dear doctor ordered?"

"If not cookies, then what will you have for dessert in your lunch tomorrow?" Mom asked.

"Nothing! I'm not some idiot child!" Gary mimed, "Have a cookie and everything will be all right." Then he clumped out of the room, leaving Brad with a familiar feeling of loss.

"Listen," Aunt Kate said, chuckling.

Clump, clump, clump-clump, clump-clump. Gary was nearly running to get away from them.

"As much as Gary hates trying to live a normal life, it's good for him," Aunt Kate said. "His mobility has improved 100% in the past three weeks."

"Yeah. But it hasn't done anything for his personality," Brad said.

"And are you a bouncing bundle of joy after hockey practice?" Aunt Kate asked. "Learning to do anything will often bring fatigue, stress, and even anguish.

"I'm surprised you're not beat, Ruth. All the months of watching over Gary. And with business booming at the shop."

Brad was leaving the room when he heard Aunt Kate say, "With Brad's hockey schedule and Gary's grouchiness, I don't know how you do stay happy, Ruth."

Oh, oh. Brad had hardly given his mom a thought since she signed his permission-to-play card.

But his mother was laughing. "Working among busy people who are buying beautiful things is my return to normal activities. It keeps me from doing too much for Gary."

The morning of the first tournament game, Brad was up, showered, and packed before either Mom or Gary stirred.

Gary made another bid to get out of going to the game. "So how does some doctor know what's good for me?" he complained. "He's never been crippled! What makes him think a guy on crutches can be happy in an arena with a group of screaming people?"

When Brad didn't answer, Gary glowered at him. "Don't you and your friends get any idea about me being water boy or anything," Gary said sarcastically.

Brad was too nervous to even notice the bite in his brother's words. Already his stomach felt as if he'd eaten Mexican jumping beans for breakfast.

Brad shouldered his hockey bag and picked up his skates, but Gary stood in front of him, leaning on his crutches. For one awful minute Brad thought Gary was going to stall things and make him late for the pregame sign-on.

"Why don't you get out of my way," Gary growled. "With all that junk hanging on you, you're more handicapped than I am."

Brad tossed his brother a set of car keys. "Then you open the tailgate for me, so I can dump this *junk* in."

Gary kept his balance by leaning on the refrigerator and right crutch and catching the keys in his left hand. Then he banged out.

Once out of the village, Brad asked, "What time is it?"

As they turned onto highway 26, he asked again.

"Two minutes since you asked the last time. For crying out loud! Stop grinning at me!" Gary snapped his head sideways to avoid seeing Brad. "You're on your way to the big game. Big deal! I'm almost 15 years old and perfectly safe staying home alone. I'm not retarded, you know! But, oh no! Big shot Brad has to drag me along. Big shot needs an audience."

Nobody answered Gary, so he went on. "But you'll wish you hadn't made me come with you! I'll stumble and fall, and embarrass you and your friends. You'll be sorry!"

"Doing things as a family is what the doctor ordered for all of us," Mother reminded the boys.

"How long does this have to go on?" Gary demanded.

"A team keeps playing as long as it keeps winning," Brad explained. "The unbeaten team gets the Class Championship and goes on to Grand Championship play."

"And if you lose today?" Gary asked, as if losing the first game was certain.

"We won't!" Brad answered confidently. "We'll score two goals in the first five minutes—the trademark of the Oak River Otters."

The Beaver Bridge Community House held not only the hockey arena, but also a gymnasium, a library, and a banquet hall-auditorium. It was host to the Summer School of Hockey, as well as Christmas and Easter tournaments.

The parking lot, though surrounded on three sides with mountainous piles of snow, was paved and snowless. *Great,* Brad thought. *Gary shouldn't slip on any ice here!*

Among the field of cars, he picked out LaBlanc's blue and white sedan, and Jerry Maloney's crew cab with his brothers and sisters piling out of it. Coach Evans and his son Tom were taking the goalie pads out of their four-year-old Ford. And

Pete, one of the new kids, was getting out of a blue Corvette.

Gametime excitement grew as the boys shouted to each other. With just one step up to the double steel and glass doors, the Phillips were in the tiled entranceway without a mishap. A huge blue and white Beaver Bridge crest was mounted on the concrete wall in front of them. The bulletin board announced Thunderland vs. Oak River, 9 A.M.

A buzz of excitement poured from the lobby beyond the crowded hall. Hockey players loaded with equipment pushed past parents who were reaching into their pockets and purses for the entrance fee.

A cashier, wearing the blue and white jacket of a Beaver Bridge hockey mother, sat behind a folding table covered with tournament programs, a cash box, date stamp, and booster buttons with team ribbons of every color.

One parent blocked the forward flow with a complaint against paying the daily entrance fee. "We're parents of the players," he grumbled. "We've already paid for the icetime in team fees." Though unhappy with the explanation of rising costs of machinery and utilities, the man paid. Gary and his mother moved up to the table.

A milkman with a red plastic basket filled with half-pint cartons of milk called out, "Coming through!"

The fee-paying group crowded together to let the delivery man pass on his way to the storeroom behind the lunch counter.

"Hey, watch it!" A boy with a cardboard box of lunch rolls held high over his head elbowed his way into the closing gap of people. "Lemme through!"

Suddenly, Gary was shoved on three sides and his crutches were pinned against the folding table. His right crutch shot out from under him, hitting the floor with the crack of hollow metal on concrete.

With a muttered curse, the bread boy fell headlong into the

people, toppling both Gary and the table. Money, schedules, and souvenirs, as well as packages of hamburger and weiner buns scattered over the floor.

"Stupid crippled kid."

Gary, who was lying in a heap on the floor, was unable to pull himself up without his crutches which were pinned under him. He lashed out the only way he could. "So I'm handicapped! But I'm not a stupid klutz that bulldozes into people!"

"Somebody's crazy for bringing a clumsy crippled kid here!" The bread boy yelled in return.

Two men in blue and white jackets of the Beaver Falls rink quickly appeared at either end of the bottlenecked entrance. One helped the bread boy take the rest of his delivery to the storeroom. The other ordered: "Please don't move until we get everything picked up."

With the championship trophy in one hand, the rink manager helped gather up the plastic packages, handfuls of cash, buttons, ribbons and schedules which littered the floor.

"You," the manager grabbed the bread boy as he returned from the storeroom. "No more barging through."

"If it hadn't been for that crippled kid dropping his crutch—" the bread boy began.

"Westbrook!" the manager interrupted, "these people are paying customers. If you can't handle deliveries any better than that, there are other bakeries in the county who can!"

Players loaded with equipment were given the right-of-way through the crowd. As Brad halted at the dressing room door, he could see that Gary had both his crutches again, was on his feet, heading toward the trophy case, as far away from the crowd as possible.

Then he saw the ice surface—larger than their home rink by at least 10 feet, with a full PA system, painted bleachers, and overhead heaters.

The jumping beans in his stomach started bouncing again

when he saw the local newsman with a TV camera. *Wow! This is it,* Brad told himself. *The first tournament for the new Oak River Otters!*

"Get with it, boys!" Coach Evans bellowed just as Brad stepped into the dressing room.

The whine of 17 bags being unzipped, the whoosh of nylon padding unfolding, and the click of metal buckles fastening— the sounds of 17 boys putting on full hockey armor, beginning with jockstrap, padding for shoulders, elbows, and shins. Then pants, sweater, socks, helmet, skates, and stick.

Seventeen sturdy 13- and 14-year-olds stalked across rubber matting like 17 miniature gladiators, armed with hickory and birch sticks and high hopes for a tournament championship.

5

 The Otters Meet the Champs

As the first red-shirted player touched ice, Oak River fans stood and cheered. Each burst of "Yea for the Otters! Hey, hey, you Big Reds" was punctuated with the clang of Katie Maloney's cowbell until all 17 boys had skated full speed around the big ice surface.

Dyn-O-mite! This is it! Brad thought. *Tournament hockey! What ice—glassy, hard, and fast!*

Brad caught sight of his mother, sitting with the Oak River fans. She was easy to spot in the white fur hat he'd given her yesterday for Christmas.

Christmas? It had never come and gone so fast before! But this year Christmas Day had been the day before tournament so—

A puck zinging past Brad's ear yanked his full attention into the pregame warm-up. The fast-paced passing, skating, and stretching was meant to tighten muscles, loosen joints, and heighten alertness.

They had to be alert!

Last year in tournament play, Brad had pulled a penalty for shooting the puck after a whistle. He wasn't about to do it

OAK RIVER OTTERS ALL-STAR TEAM

NUMBER	NAME	POSITION
1	Tom "Chug" Evans	Goalie
2	Mark LaBlanc	Right defense
3	Andy Farrell	Left wing
4	Brad Phillips	Left defense
5	Kurt Carpenter	Right defense
6	Don MacDougal	Left defense
7	Carl "Flip" Sawyer	Left wing
8	Danny Martin	Right wing
9	Jerry Maloney	Centerman
10	Tim Johnson	Left wing
11	Danny Holden	Right wing
12	Pete Peters	Centerman
14	Mike Rawleigh	Right wing
15	Steve Woods	Left defense
16	Keith Redman	Left wing
17	Sam Endachuck	Right defense
30	Gord Thompson	Goalie

OFFICIALS

Coach: Art Evans

Manager: Joe LaBlanc

Team Captain: Mark LaBlanc

Team Assistant Captains:

Brad Phillips

Jerry Maloney

again. Two minutes in the "sin bin" [8] could cause the team to lose a tight game.

The referee skated out. The whistle blew. Five green-shirted players and five reds glided to face-off [9] position at center ice. Twelve heads went up. Twelve sticks went down. The whistle blew. The puck dropped.

Jerry scooped the first face-off, but was checked off three feet from the center circle. It took a winger, Flip #7, and two defensemen, Brad #4 and Mark #2, the full length of the ice to get it back. Mark jabbed it out of the goal crease, passed to Brad who slammed it up the boards to Flip who was already heading to the Thunderland blue line.

Slap! The puck was deflected by the Thunderland goalie.

From the first three minutes of play, all five Otters on the ice knew Thunderland was a stronger team than they'd ever met before. From that first smack of wood on rubber, the green-shirted Thunderland players skated as fast as speed skaters and passed with deadly aim.

All five Otters skated, checked, and passed, but the Thunderland defense held unshaken. The green goalie wielded his stick and glove with the speed and cunning of a sleight-of-hand artist. He shut out every shot the Otters slammed his way.

Oak River didn't score two goals in the first five minutes of play as Brad had predicted.

But neither did Thunderland!

Lines changed and rechanged. The game picked up speed as play swung up and down the full length of the ice with the regularity of a pendulum on a well-wound grandfather clock.

The officials in black-and-white striped shirts skated around

---

[8] *Sin bin* is another name for the penalty box.

[9] *Face-off*: The puck is held by the referee and dropped to the face-off dot on the ice to begin play. At the beginning of a period, or after one team has scored, face-off goes to center circle.

the action, or hung from the boards to let play pass as they whistled down the offsides [10] and double-line passes.[11]

The Thunderland fans all stood as their team snatched control of the puck, but sank back to the bleachers as the Oak River fans rose to cheer when their team regained control.

When the whistle blew to end the first period, the large electric scoreboard still flashed 0-0.

Coach Evans eyed the line of numbered red helmets before him on the dressing room bench. "OK, boys. You played a good first period. You held last year's champions to a scoreless game. But you can't win unless you score!"

Then, like the hockey coach and father he was, he laid it all out: "It'll get harder to score as the game goes on. They've got a second and third string as strong as their first. You've got to score now. You've got to go for the hole in their defense. Get out there and make them make a mistake. Then get that puck in the net!" He was almost pleading. "That's not too much to ask of a hockey team, now is it?"

Five goal-hungry Otters dashed through the door and skated to center circle for face-off.

By halftime of the second period it was evident that both teams were equally determined to gain a winner's spot in tournament play.

But fatigue was the Otters' real enemy. Here the time clock was tipped in Thunderland's favor since it had greater team depth.

Coach Evans turned to Brad who was resting on the bench. "Got your wind back?"

Brad nodded.

"OK, numbers 4, 5, 9, 7, 14. Get out there and skate up a storm in that Thunderland zone!"

---

[10] *Offside:* When a player crosses into the opposing zone ahead of the puck. The referee whistles for a face-off.

[11] *Double-line pass:* When the puck is passed across two lines before being intercepted by another player. This gets a whistle and a face-off too.

Brad nodded. But he didn't like playing the blue line [12] with Kurt #5, who never checked unless checked first. So who did the coach stick him with? The new kid, #5.

Crumb, Brad grumbled to himself. *On the ice with a teammate who won't play defensively!* Kurt played hockey as if he were at a garden party. He was skating better and his stickhandling was so-so, but Kurt was body-contact shy. He wouldn't check!

No way could they win this game without the defense checking and checking and checking. Especially with Thunderland winger #11 on the ice. There was no way around him. He was as tricky as greased lightning and just as fast!

Brad had sweated through one and a half periods of scoreless play with Thunderland. He knew that if the Otters were ever going to put the puck in the net, they'd have to go right through Thunderland's defense and risk a tripping penalty if **one** of its players fell.

The referee held the puck over the red dot, glanced around to see five Green players and five Reds in face-off position. He dropped it.

Crack! A Thunderland winger rammed Flip from behind, driving him to the ice.

The whistle blew and the striped arm waved two new players in for a face-off.

Brad saw the white #9 which always looked so big on Jerry's slight back, caught the tilt of his red helmet, and smiled. Brad shifted his stance, waiting to receive Jerry's left-handed slice. Something Thunderland didn't know—Oak River's #9 was ambidextrous. He could pass and shoot equally well either left or right.

Slam! Brad received the puck and passed it all in one

---

[12] *Battle at the blue line* is sometimes called "play at the point." It refers to the placing of a defenseman just inside the opposing team's blue line, near the boards. A forward or another defenseman who doesn't have an opening to shoot will try to get the puck to that defenseman for a direct shot at the goal.

action, zinging it across the ice to Kurt, who passed to Flip.

The Otters were on the move! Otter fans rose to shout, "Go, boys, go!"

Jerry skated stride for stride with Flip. Brad drove to cut off Thunderland's #8 before he could split the two-man rush, leaving the Green #2 for Kurt to handle.

Flip carried the puck across the blue line well into the Thunderland left zone, but was checked off it by Green #2, ahead of Kurt.

Flip went down, taking the Thunderland player with him.

Kurt poked the puck loose and backpassed to Brad who shot it across to Jerry on right wing.

Jerry leaned right to receive, drawing the green goalie with him. Quickly he shifted his weight and slammed a left-handed shot right into the net. A goal!

The Oak River Otters huddled to back-slap each other all the way to the bench for a line change.

"Yea! Yea, you Big Reds!" The fans cheered again and again.

The PA crackled: Goal for Oak River scored by #9, Jerry Maloney. Assist #4, Brad Phillips and #7, Flip Sawyer. The time 12 minutes and 45 seconds.

The roar of Otter fans and Katie Maloney's cowbell drowned out all other sound.

The Oak River Reds, the unknowns in tournament play, had scored the first goal!

Coach Evans slapped each player on the rump as he came off the ice, but eyed each anxiously. Knowing Thunderland would come out braced for a comeback, he sent out numbers 2, 4, 6, 11, 17.

Thunderland won the face-off.

Already moving backward, Brad braced for the right second to move up on the puck carrier. Thank God, Mark was there. If Brad took one man, Mark could hold the other. Flip would take care of the puck.

Crash! Brad caught the intended slap shot on his shin pads, caught the puck with his stick, and passed to Mark.

Thunderland #2 zoomed out of neutral zone, intercepted the puck with a slap shot straight on goal.

Ting! Saved by the crossbar! Brad groaned in relief and rushed back of the net to kill any rebound. Instantly he was rammed against the boards by two Greens. It was all he could do to freeze the puck [13] for a face-off.

When the whistle sounded to end play, one Green released him. But the other jerked his stick, as if to free it, but instead he jabbed Brad hard enough to jolt his teeth into his eyeballs.

"Turkey? You OK?" Mark yelled as he rushed over to look. Katie Maloney leaned over the boards shouting for a butt-ending [14] penalty. The ref crouched for face-off in Oak River's end, turning a deaf ear to everything off the ice.

Brad saw Green #11 and #2. Didn't they ever take those two off the ice? Coach Evans sent out a fresh line to face the drop in their zone. Even so, it was a dangerous—

Whistle. Crack! Crack!

Up went the Thunderland sticks. Round and round went the Thunderland cheers. The PA crackled: Goal by Thunderland #2, Walker, Assist by #11 Stephensen.

Straight from the face-off to the goal in two moves, before the Oak River boys had even touched the puck.

"We'll get it back," Mark promised as he whacked Chug on his well-padded rump. But the five red players headed to the bench with shoulders sagging, heads too heavy to hold up.

"We've *got* to get it back," Brad said through clenched teeth. *And we will,* he promised himself, knowing Gary was out there hoping they'd lose.

---

[13] *Freezing the puck:* A player jams the puck against the boards to stop play and force a face-off. If done without an opposing player moving into battle for it, it can result in a penalty.

[14] *Butt-ending* is using the shaft end of the hockey stick to jab another player. It calls for a two-minute penalty.

Nothing mattered now but the action on the ice. The cheerers, the hecklers and the TV newsman's camera were all forgotten as action tightened to a hysterical pace. Whistles blew; lines changed.

Play was into the third period now and Coach Evans started substituting players freely. When play shifted toward the Thunderland net, he pulled out a defenseman and sent in an extra winger.

Try as they might, Oak River wasn't coming close to scoring. All Katie's cowbell clanging and all the rousing cheers by the Otter fans couldn't crack the power of the Thunderland Greens.

"Hey, Turkey!" Mark screamed.

Brad swung to meet the oncoming puck with a powerful slap. It zinged high. The crowd gasped in surprise.

Ting! It caught the goalpost and spun outward from the net. Their goalie pounced on it, killing Pete's chance for a rebound shot.

Brad sat out his rest period on the bench, all his body working to breathe deeply. But fatigue hadn't conquered him yet. He felt a furry dryness in his mouth, tasting only the coppery gut urge to win.

They could win, Brad believed. Oak River, the unknowns, had drawn last year's champions for their first game. But they could win! With a 1-1 tie and 5 minutes and 19 seconds to go, it was anybody's game!

Suddenly, the Oak River fans came alive, yelling: "Go, Mike go!"

Mike Rawleigh, Otter #14, had a breakaway.

Two greens crossed the ice from either side, two strides ahead of any red men. Mike pitched forward over a green-taped stick.

"Trip! Trip! Trip!" Oak River fans called for a penalty.

The ref cut his open palm across his lower leg. The PA

called it. Thunderland #8, Cheasley, two minutes for tripping.

While the referees recorded the penalty, Coach Evans explained to the boys: It's got to be a win. If there's a tie at the end of regulation time, the game goes into sudden death overtime and first goal wins. An overtime [15] is a tough way to win a game—and a tougher way to lose it. You've got 4 minutes and 42 seconds to do it up right!

Thunderland sent out four powerful penalty killers for their two minutes of shorthanded play.[16]

Oak River sent out Brad, Mark, Flip, Jerry, and Pete, with the coach's bellow ringing in their ears, "Don't let them wind up!"

Oak River had the man advantage but Thunderland lined up four abreast looking as invincible as a formation of dive-bombers moving in two by two.

Pete won the face-off. Two Greens moved in: one for the man, one for the puck. The other two started toward the Oak River net, spaced wide but not far enough to risk an offside pass.

Brad edged backwards, watching closely for the shift in body weight—the telltale move before a shot. It didn't come. At the last second Brad dived, knowing he'd take the puck carrier with him. Was he too late? He waited those awful two seconds. It came—like a bomb exploding in his ears.

Thunderland had scored a shorthanded goal—2-1 for Thunderland. Only four minutes remained in the game.

Brad sank onto the bench exhausted, hurting inside where fatigue hadn't yet reached. *If Gary—No. Gary isn't in this game,* Brad told himself. *It's me, #4, who let that shot*

---

[15] *Overtime* is a period of play required to determine a winner when regulation time ends with a tie score.

[16] Playing *shorthanded:* A team must play less a player if one has a penalty. Less two players if two have penalties. If three players draw penalties, the third penalty is delayed and served after the first penalty expires. A team is not required to play with less than four players.

through. Slowly his breathing slowed to a normal pace. The whistle blew. Coach Evans gave him the nod.

"One goal at a time boys. One right now will get us a tie. Buy us some time, boys!"

Pete scooped the face-off to Flip who skirted the Thunderland wingers, dipped through their defense, and backpassed to Pete just outside their blue line.

Pete carried the puck into Thunderland's zone, then he hesitated.

Go, man, go, Brad screamed to himself, *before you get creamed.* Thunderland's double checking could make peanut butter out of Pete.

Crash! Brad lost sight of Pete. He couldn't tell whether the crack had been shoulder pads or helmets.

Pete was through the blockade. Thunderland #8 and #11 had checked each other! Pete was through! He shot! He scored!

Pete scored!

Brad danced up and down on the blue line. The TV cameras were getting shots of the fans screaming. Nobody heard the PA announcer above Katie's cowbell. Cheer rolled on cheer. Red players slapped and hugged each other. Coach Evans cackled aloud, "Their goalie thought Pete was taken out of play. That kid's a blooming figure skater! One more goal, boys! Just one more!"

Less than two minutes to go and it was still anybody's game. Fatigue forgotten, the Otters lined up for the last line of play in regulation time.

The Greens won the face-off. Flip skated in, flipped his attacker, swung the puck left, and passed to Mike just outside Thunderland's blue line. Brad moved up with the action, making sure he kept the big Green #11 well within stick range.

Each team drove for the puck, hard and fast, hungry for that goal that would give it a win.

Once, twice, Brad and Mark cut Thunderland off at the blue line before the Greens could wind up for a shot.

With one minute to go, a deliberate double-line pass by Thunderland brought a face-off back inside their blue line.

The whistle shrilled. Play headed for the Oak River end. Brad skated backwards, his stick ranging left to right just above the ice, discouraging any forward movement of the Greens toward the boards.

He caught the puck by the tip of his stick, spinning it weakly away from a goal shot. Pete swooped in to start a reverse rush, but play was fouled at the blue line, as Thunderland poke-checked the puck into an offside for a whistle.

Thunderland pulled their goalie and sent out six attackers. With four seconds to go, the tension was almost unbearable.

Jerry won the face-off and swung the puck back to Brad, who lifted his arm for a hard pass. He heard a whistle and automatically let his arm drop. His mind didn't reason why, his muscles acted automatically at the sound.

But play didn't stop.

That second of hesitation was all Thunderland needed to steal the puck and slam it into the Oak River net.

The time buzzer was lost in the shouts of Thunderland players and fans. Green helmets, mitts and sticks cluttered the ice as the Thunderland players smothered each other with congratulations.

"Hey, Turkey?" Mark was the first to reach Brad. "You had it! You gave it away! Why?"

"I heard a whistle! Didn't you hear it?" Brad asked.

Flip, Chug, and Mark looked at him as if he'd gone crazy.

I know I heard a whistle. I thought play was called. Brad was still saying it to himself when Mark came back from talking to the referees.

"Too late. Play was called. The game is over."

Thunderland won, 3-2.

There was nothing to do but line up, shake hands, and ignore their jeers and taunts. But Thunderland's jeers were tame to what Gary would say.

Brad's sweat-streaked face burned with fresh misery. His stomach churned with self-blame. He was about to believe he'd imagined that whistle when Thunderland #11 hissed through teeth bared in a sneering victory grin: "Sucker!"

He hadn't imagined it after all! There *had* been an illegal whistle!

"What did you say?" Brad demanded.

"I said you've got a lot to learn about tournament hockey, sucker!"

So his ears hadn't failed him. *But his good sense had!* He lost the team a chance at overtime. He, Brad Phillips, who needed a win as much, or more than anyone else on the team!

Brad skated to the dressing room as if he had lead in his blades. All the fatigue he hadn't felt during play weighed him down.

Brad Phillips, all-star player, beaten on a slap shot with three seconds to go in a tie game!

He slumped onto the bench, too tired to wrestle with soaked pads and tight laces. The dressing room was deathly silent.

6

A Thief in the Crowd

The Oak River Otters had stalked across the rubber matting from the ice to the dressing room with smiles that said, "So we lost. But you'll not catch us crying."

After the first few minutes the silence in the dressing room broke. "What happened, Brad? You handed the game to them! You had the chance to send the game into overtime! You gave it away!"

"Brad, how could *you?*" Mark demanded.

"I blew it! I know!" Brad sputtered, defensively. "But if a couple of you guys had scored, my goof wouldn't have mattered. Don't blame it all on me."

Coach Evans let out a bellow. "You're a team! You play together! You win together! You lose together! Today you lost. But you're not losers until you blame someone else!"

Seventeen boys watched silently as their coach pointed out Game 2 on the tournament chart. "Elmwood vs. Shale Bay— they're out there on the ice now," Coach Evans pointed out. "We play the loser tomorrow at 9 A.M. Thunderland will play the winner tomorrow at 10 A.M.

"We're not out yet," the coach emphasized. "As long as we

54

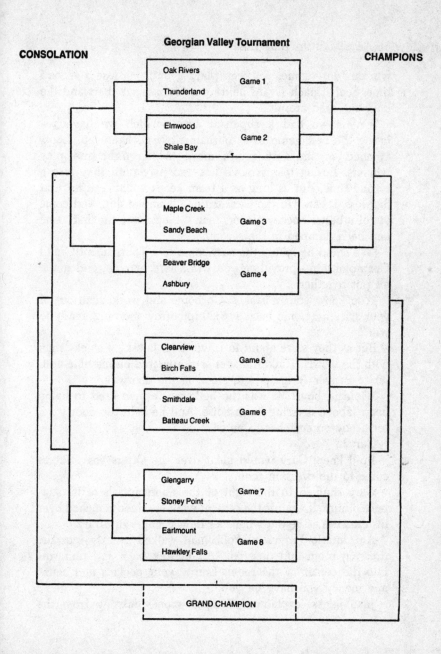

Georgian Valley Tournament

CONSOLATION

CHAMPIONS

Oak Rivers
Thunderland
Game 1

Elmwood
Shale Bay
Game 2

Maple Creek
Sandy Beach
Game 3

Beaver Bridge
Ashbury
Game 4

Clearview
Birch Falls
Game 5

Smithdale
Batteau Creek
Game 6

Glengarry
Stoney Point
Game 7

Earlmount
Hawkley Falls
Game 8

GRAND CHAMPION

win our next game, we keep playing until we lose a second time. See!" Coach Evans held up a tournament chart and the boys gathered around.

"Unless we had a superstar team—which we haven't—losing the first game in a tournament is no handicap. Look. Winners of the first games move to the right and play winners. Losing teams move left and play until they lose a second time. But as long as a team keeps winning, *after* that first loss, it can win the Consolation Championship, and come out of it better hockey players than if they'd won the first game and been dumped in the second.

"We could be taking the easy route to a Tournament Grand Championship—providing you work hard enough, and get it all put together.

"You know your mistakes. Go home and work them out of your systems. Come back at 8:30 tomorrow morning, ready to win!"

But as they were about to leave, Jake Jaleski, a stocky man with the words "Rink Manager" embroidered on his blue-and-white Beaver Ridge jacket, stood in the doorway.

"Hold it, boys!" It was the bellow of a man used to being heard above dressing room noise. And he held the door open for a boy on crutches to enter.

Gary?

Brad knew Gary would gloat over the Otters' loss, but to come to the dressing room . . .

Gary shuffled to the right of the doorway where he supported himself against the cement wall. He stood hunched over his crutches as he did whenever he was angry or afraid.

An Ontario Provincial Policeman walked quickly into the dressing room and ordered, "All hockey bags and uniforms into the center of the room. Empty your pockets and count any money you have on you."

Jake Jaleski explained: "There's money missing from the

cash table. The Thunderland and Oak River teams were checking in when the table was turned over. Two hundred dollars is missing."

The Otters, beaten and dead tired two minutes before, suddenly came alive. They whipped off sweaters, socks, and pads and tossed them on top of their hockey bags in the center of the room, then stood in sweat-soaked T-shirts and long johns, watching the search with the eagerness of young boys playing cops and robbers. Only this was a real cop looking for real money—in the Oak River all-star dressing room!

The only bulges they found on the boys were the normal battle scars of a tough hockey game: a few purple bruises and some swollen flesh.

"Hey!" The policeman held up a red leather bag with the initials P.P. and a Montreal Canadians crest on it. "I didn't know you had Peter Paquette, the NHL's star centerman, playing for you?"

The boys laughed. Mark said, "We wouldn't have lost that game if he played for the Otters!"

"That's my bag, sir," Pete said, his face turning red.

"Whose bags are these?" The officer held up two sports bags, one red, one brown.

Flip pointed to the red nylon one with an Otter crest on it. Kurt claimed the brown one. "Mine, sir."

"OK, boys, get dressed. You're free to go—except for you three." He pointed to Flip, Kurt, and Gary.

Gary braced his back against the wall, as if he were trying to fade into the gray concrete and get out of the questioning.

Though free to go, Brad stayed behind, wondering why Gary was being questioned.

The investigating officer turned to Gary. "You were there. Tell us what happened."

"I told you," Gary began, sullenly. "I didn't see anything happen. I was shoved from behind by that bread boy."

"I checked the Westbrook boy on his way out," the rink manager said.

"Who else was within reach of the money?" the policeman asked Gary.

"My brother." He pointed with his chin at Brad. "He's always around when I go somewhere for the first time. But I didn't see him. I didn't see anything. When that bread boy shoved me into the table, I went down and everything was on top of me. I told you, you don't get a good view on the floor with stuff falling all over you. If you ask me, it was that dumb delivery kid."

But it was Brad Gary glowered at. Gary's eyes snapped out all the unsaid, angry things—"So you got it your way. You dragged me here to see the big hockey heroes. Instead, I saw a bunch of losers. I told you I'd stumble and embarrass you and your friends. You'll be sorry!"

Brad squirmed under Gary's scalding stare and thought, *Gary doesn't know or care that I hurt too. He doesn't care about anyone except himself.*

"Sure I knew there was money on that table," Gary was saying to the officer. "Mother had just paid my way in. But why drag me in here? I don't have a hockey bag to hide $200 in! And where would I hide money on me?" Gary patted his loose-fitting corduroy pants and bulky-knit sweater. Neither had buckles or pockets that might catch the movement of his body between crutches.

The policeman turned away from Gary, and Brad watched Gary hobble out of the dressing room. By then most of the boys had dressed, packed, and left. Brad got up and into his clothes as the officer spoke to Kurt and Flip.

"Between you two boys, you have over $200 in your bags. Isn't that a lot of money for a kid to carry to a hockey game?"

"Nobody knew we had it, sir," Kurt said, "until you made us

turn out our stuff. Who expects a kid to have money?"

"That's just it,' the policeman hurried to make his point. "Almost any kid has pop and hot dog money. Some even have enough cash to sharpen skates or replace a hockey stick. But $200 between you? So tell me why?"

"I always carry money. Nobody knows it. Now I won't be able to, will I?" Kurt's usual agreeable manner suddenly turned sullen. He was new to the Oak River team and the area.

The policeman ignored him now and turned to Flip. "The name on the sign-on sheet is Carl. The name on your bag is Flip."

"So? My name is Carl. Everyone calls me Flip. On by birth certificate I'm registered as Carl Wolfgang Sawyer. My mother favors her German family names. As for me, Flip will do."

Brad wondered why Flip didn't tell the officer his dad was in the Ontario Provincial Police too. Instead, Flip chuckled as he continued to sound like a character on a TV cops and robbers show.

"I have money because I have a paper route for the Toronto Star. I have two weeks' collection on me," Flip concluded.

"What's your reason?" The policeman swung back to Kurt who just shrugged. "C'mon now. I saw that last period. You kids played a tough game. You proved you're coolheaded, quick thinkers. You don't *just happen* to do anything. I think you have a good reason for carrying more than 100 bucks on you, even if the dressing room is locked all the time."

Kurt sat glum-faced, saying nothing.

"OK, then you've got a *bad* reason!" The policeman was growing impatient. "You saw that bundle of bills fall off the table, and in the mad scramble you saw your chance to get away with it unnoticed. You had enough time to stuff the bills in your wallet in the dressing room before the game."

"With 16 other guys watching?"

"There's a walled-off area over there." The policeman

pointed to the private booths in the shower room portion of the dressing room.

Still Kurt waited.

"OK, kid. Do I write down that you refuse to answer, then phone your mother?"

Kurt looked up, startled. "You wouldn't!"

"So your mother doesn't know you carry this kind of money around to hockey games? Did you steal it from her purse?"

"No! It's mine!"

The policeman sat down beside Kurt on the bench and leaned back as if prepared for a long seige.

Finally Kurt got up and finished dressing. When he was done, he shrugged and said, "My dad gave it to me."

"Your mother and dad are divorced?" the officer suggested.

"None of your business!" Kurt snapped at the policeman.

Brad, now fully dressed and packed, had no reason to hang around the dressing room any longer. He left and worked his way through the crowd in the lobby to the wall-sized chart of the tournament schedule. He looked at the upcoming teams, trying to calculate the Otters' chances of winning their way all the way down the losing side to the Grand Championship Game. Two boys in blue-and-white jackets pushed in front of Brad.

"I was hoping Oak River would dump Thunderland— they're trouble!" one said. "Then we could take the Otters. Boy, are they lousy! Did you see them in that third period? Did you see how that clumsy defenseman gave the puck away with only three seconds to go!"

Brad tried to duck out of sight, but bumped into someone. He turned to apologize and found himself face to face with Pete, who was grinning.

Brad whispered, "You wouldn't think it was funny if it had happened to you!"

"You take life too seriously," Pete said, still smiling. "Everybody gets shot down sometime in a team sport. Tomorrow's a new game."

"You really don't care if you get beat?"

"Sure I care, I like playing and I like winning. But sometimes you learn more from the losses than from the wins," Pete said.

Brad looked squarely at Pete, now out of his hockey equipment. He hadn't paid much attention to him, except to know that he was the only new kid who could outskate guys like Jerry, Flip, Mark, and himself.

"Where'd you learn to skate like that?" Brad asked, as they walked the long hallway to the parking lot.

"At the school I went to last year. I had figure skating in gym class."

"Wow! Where'd you find a school like that? Not around here?"

"Nah. Wasn't as much fun as here. Lessons for this and lessons for that. And if you didn't do everything perfect the instructors acted as if you were a failure," Pete said, laughing.

Brad had never heard Pete laugh before.

"My skating instructor would've died if he'd heard Coach Evan's cackle over that lousy dive I took. He sounded like a hen that'd just laid a square egg."

Pete's mother waved to him across the crowded hall. Brad thought she looked more like an older sister, home from the city for the weekend, than an Oak River mother.

"See you tomorrow," Pete said. "Same time, same place— different scoreboard." He was still laughing to himself as he ducked out into the cold.

Brad heard Gary's crutch steps coming across the rubber mat behind him. "All frisked and questioned," he said. "Not fingerprinted yet. But they have to arrest me to do that, don't they?" When alongside Brad he added, "I knew your friends were hoodlums, but thieves?"

"Boys!" Mother warned, coming up behind them. She nodded toward the door.

Once settled in the car, Gary sneered. "Where's your Christianity now, little brother? You know all that stuff you and the good people of the church believe about not standing with sinners and not sitting with the scornful. Remember, it was your friends who got me questioned and searched by police—like a common thief."

When finally headed for home on the bare band of pavement between parallel snowbanks, Gary growled. "What a lot of flak just to lose one lousy hockey game!"

Brad was too tired to explain the scheduling, so tossed his program into the back seat.

Mom spoke up then: "Isn't Peter an odd name for parents to call a boy with the last name Peters? And Mrs. Peters seems like such a nice person, not one to play a trick like that on a child—Peter Peters."

"Hey. I never thought of it that way," Brad said. "The kids just call him Pete. But put together: Peter Peters does sound funny."

"How about some heat back here," Gary demanded. "My feet are frozen from that arena."

"Everybody feels the cold in an arena," Mom answered, as she turned the heater fan to high.

Brad sank into his own fatigue-fogged thoughts. How could anything he'd worked for so long, be over so fast. If they lost again it would be all over tomorrow.

"It's much more interesting in the bleachers. You can hear the action," his mother said. "There are overhead heaters. And your feet are off the concrete floor. It's really warmer out there."

Suddenly Brad sat up straighter, wondering if he'd heard right. His mother was actually treating Gary like a normal person! Maybe there would be no more special treatment—no more soundproof helmet and face mask to everything but Gary's needs.

"I might have known," Gary grumbled. "You're turning into a hockey mother!"

Ruth Phillips laughed. "Not yet. See! No cowbell! But Julia Peters did tell me about boot warmers used by figure skaters. They're made of fur and zip on over leather boots. They'd keep your feet warm—"

"Oh great! Now I'm the topic of a hockey mothers' gossip group!"

"That's enough, Gary," Mother said quietly, yet firmly.

"Hey, Mom?" Brad asked. "Is she really Pete's mother?"

"Beautiful isn't she? And such a gentle person."

"Just give her time! She'll turn into a cowbell clanging mama too!" Gary tossed the schedule onto the front seat. "This routine could go on for the whole Christmas vacation. What a lousy way to spend the holidays!"

Brad said it before his brother could. "Maybe you'll get lucky, and we'll lose tomorrow."

"Fat chance! I saw Elmwood and Shale Bay playing while you were getting dressed. They're *both* lousier than you guys!"

Later, as Brad told Aunt Kate about his first game in tournament play, he said, "We lost the game, but Coach Evans says we're not losers until we blame someone else."

"That's something worth learning, nephew of mine," she answered.

"Thunderland doesn't know how fast we can learn," Brad said, as he explained the scheduling and the possibility of meeting them again in the Grand Championship final game.

Mom told her of the mix-up that ended with the dumped table and stolen money. "Two deliveries came in—a milkman and a bread boy. The bread boy, Robby Westbrook, had plenty to say."

"I heard him, loud and clear," Gary said. "He called me a

crippled kid on crutches. I told him that any kid that'd barge through people the way he did had something worse than crutches bugging him!"

. Aunt Kate smiled at Gary, then turned and winked at Brad.

Gary was eating gumdrop cookies and drinking hot chocolate as he talked. "And I told that overgrown boy scout in the hockey jacket that his crummy 200 bucks wasn't enough to make a thief out of me. If I was going to steal, I'd be smart enough to wait until 9 P.M. and get the whole day's take. Only an idiot would rob an arena in the morning!"

"Oh Gary, was that a wise thing to say?" his mother asked. "That arena must take in over $1000 a day during tournament. What if there should be such a theft?"

Brad heard the concern in his mother's voice. Did Mom remember Gary's threat? *You'll be sorry you dragged me along.* Did she wonder, as he did, if Gary could have taken the money?

That night, as Brad tossed back the blankets on his bed and turned on his lamp to read, he asked himself, *What does a guy do when he suspects his brother of stealing? Ask him? But that's accusing, isn't it? And on what grounds?*

He had a feeling that Gary knew more than he was telling. Was there some way to look for evidence? Nah, boy detectives belonged in books like the Hardy Boys series, not in real families and tournament hockey.

Mr. Jaleski said he had searched the delivery boy on the way out. And Gary certainly had no way of carrying money. The two hockey teams had been checked too.

He thought then about the Otters. What did he really know about them? He'd gone all through school with Mark, Chug, Jerry, and Flip, but he knew little about the others. And the ones he knew the least—Sam, Pete, and Kurt—had the most money to spend. So why would they steal?

Brad groaned. *This is dumb,* he thought, *me lying here*

picking my brother apart—and the team—when I have to play a do-or-die game with them first thing in the morning! A guy can't play good hockey with fellows he doesn't trust.

Just before he went to sleep, he prayed—simply: *Lord, help me not to be suspicious and resentful of Gary—or my teammates. I know You said we shouldn't judge. Bring me through this temptation. Thanks! Amen.*

Dyn-O-mite! It came to him as he finished praying: He couldn't spy on his brother or his teammates. But he could look for the money!

Dyn-O-mite! That was it! The money! It flew off the table when the table was toppled. But it didn't keep flying. It landed somewhere. Maybe someone found it and hid it. Tomorrow, first thing, he'd be back at the scene of the crime. He could hardly wait to get back.

Finally, Brad slept.

7

 # Brad Turns
Detective

Either the second drive to Beaver Bridge arena went faster than the first, or else Brad had too many things on his mind to ask what time it was more than twice.

He watched snowflakes landing on the windshield as he tried to sort it all out. Getting the question straight inside his head—not *who's* the thief but *where's* the money—was one thing. Getting an answer to that question was quite another.

"Worried about this team?" Mom asked as she pulled into the parking lot of the arena.

"Elmwood? Nah! The Shale Bay Bears put them out into consolation play, and the Bears haven't won a game with us yet this year. Nothing to worry about there."

Brad pulled his gear from the back of the station wagon and caught up with Gary at the wide glass doors. Once inside the arena, he noticed that yesterday's folding table was replaced with a sturdy wooden one. Two women in rink jackets sat at it, one taking entrance fees, the other selling programs and team buttons.

Brad looked around the glassed-in lobby. *Where would*

someone drop a bundle of bills in a hurry? A place they could get to after the police left? Where's a private spot in a public arena?

The washroom! Where else?

That cut Brad's search in half, since one washroom was out of bounds to him. He dropped his bag in dressing room 4 and ducked out before the team could get him into a pregame discussion.

The "can," like everything else in Beaver Bridge, was painted blue and white.

Brad lifted a big plastic bag out of a trash container to see what it contained. It wasn't money.

One by one, he checked behind the plumbing in each stall.

"Hey Turkey!" Mark burst in. "How many toilets are you trying out?" Sudden alarm squeezed his freckles together. "You're not catching the flu bug?"

"No! It's nothing like that." Then Brad explained his suspicions and his search.

"But why here?" Mark wanted to know.

"Can you think of a better place to hide money?"

"But the police went through here yesterday like a two-man bomb squad after a bomb threat. Anyway, what's it to you?"

"It's just—" Brad looked at his freckled friend, and without really intending to, he said, "Someone from either Oak River or Thunderland must have taken the money."

Then he told Mark about his concern for Gary: "Gary is here because of me. He hates every minute of it and he warned me he'd stumble and embarass me. Well, he did stumble. He fell right over the table of dumped money."

As the door to the last stall banged behind Brad, he faced his friend in the otherwise empty lavatory and admitted, "Isn't that awful? Thinking that about my brother? And I call myself a Christian!"

"What's that got to do with it?" Mark demanded. "A guy's

got to trust his instincts about people. Couldn't be a good hockey player if he didn't!"

Flip slammed through the door. "Why aren't you guys dressing?"

"Just casing the joint for some 'found money.' " Mark said.

"Forget it!" Flip answered. "That money's long gone, in some parent's purse or hip pocket!"

"Parent?" Brad and Mark chorused.

"Sure! Not all parents are squares like yours," Flip declared. "I know! My Dad's a policeman. And every time I try to collect money from parents on my paper route, one or another tries to gyp me out of a dollar or two. Believe me, guys, some parent is having a happy holiday on that money."

With that remark, the three boys rushed to the dressing room. They unzipped, buckled, snapped, and tied their hockey equipment with movements so familiar they could do it in their sleep.

As they lined up for the long march across the rubber matting to the gate, their coach spoke to them. "Any team who thinks it has its competition beaten before it gets wood on rubber is on its way to losing," he began. "Now, get out there and play good hockey!"

Seventeen red helmets, all in a row. Seventeen sticks held upright by seventeen eager Otters. Mark #2 leaned back to talk to Brad #4, "Flip's probably right about the money. But if it's bugging you that much, I'll check with my cousin Steve after the game. He's working at the refreshment stand today and knows what's going on."

The whistle blew.

Seventeen sets of steel blades cut ice. Seventeen red-shirted warriors in plastic armor flashed around the ice in stretching strides.

They looked good, and the fans responded. If a team could be judged by its cheering section, the Otters had the edge on

Elmwood—even before Katie Maloney brought out her cow-bell.

The referee crouched for the drop. The red helmets zoomed from one end of the rink, and the orange helmets from the other to face-off position at center ice.

The Otters' first string braced themselves for a fast start—heads up, sticks down.

Jerry scooped the first face-off to Flip who whizzed up the boards and passed the full width of the ice to Pete who carried the puck across the blue line. Pete quickly drop-passed [17] to Flip for a fast left-sided shot.

They scored, nine seconds into the game. 1-0 for the Oak River Otters.

The second drop of the puck at center went to Elmwood who backpassed to the orange shirt Brad was shadowing.

"Hey Turkey," Flip yelped, as Brad sliced the puck away from the orangeman's stick. He carried it a few strides, then passed up to the blue line just ahead of Flip, who drove forward with it and scored!

Two goals in the first two shots on goal! Dyn-O-mite!

That took care of any of the Otters' leftover blues from yesterday. Coach Evans strutted up and down the box, cackling to himself like a hen that just laid a double-yolked egg. "That's what I've been telling you! Get in there and score in the first period. Then the third period's no sweat!"

The Oak River fans kept the rafters ringing for 20 seconds with the chant, "Do it again, do it again."

Elmwood changed teams, sending out a determined-looking five, their orange helmets thrust forward from set shoulders.

Play moved into the Elmwood zone. Brad and Mark picked their spots just inside the blue line. At the first move of the

---

[17] *Drop pass:* The puck carrier moves forward, leaving the puck for a teammate who is trailing him. Done in a close-checking game to keep the opposition from capturing the puck.

puck to Brad, an Elmwood winger checked hard but bounced off the stance of the sturdy Oak River defenseman.

The next pass, the same Elmwood winger took a flying leap that spoiled Brad's slap shot, but drew a charging penalty in return.

At the end of the first period of play, the Otters had 14 shots on goal, to the Orange 3, and the scoreboard lighted up at 7-0 for Oak River.

On his rest shift, late in second period, Brad noticed an empty seat in the bleachers beside Pete's mother. Then he saw his mother returning with two white cups in hand. She wasn't a coffee drinker, at least not from styrofoam cups. And she claimed no arena made a decent cup of tea. Yet she'd gone out to the lunch counter in the hall where Gary usually stood. Did she wonder about him too?

At the whistle, Brad got up to return to the ice. Coach waved him down and sent out Mike, Danny, Kurt, and Don— a line he hadn't used before.

Kurt let a puck through the blue line. Don recovered it and drop-passed to Danny who was standing right in front of the slot. The first-year centerman reacted and scored his first goal of the season.

As Oak River's score grew, so did the coach's nervousness. He grumbled aloud about their increasingly sloppy playing: "Games are won or lost at the blue line. With this team you can recover. Pete and Jerry can outskate any Elmwood player. But if this had been Thunderland, that slip would have cost us a goal.

"See what I'm telling you!" Coach Evans paced up and down the box. "Games are won and lost at the blue line!" He tapped Brad on the helmet. "Kurt's playing too far in. He's leaving the blue line undefended. Sure he's hungry for a goal. What hockey player isn't? But he's supposed to be playing defense.

"Pass! Pass!" Coach shouted at Danny flying by the boards. "This is a team sport, not a speed-skating race." Coach continued to agonize over their runaway win as much as he had over yesterday's loss. "A game like this is good for morale, but bad for team play. You guys should be putting new plays into your game, not this sloppy, slaphappy scrimmaging!"

With five minutes to go in the game, and an 11-goal lead, Coach sent out Brad and Mark to defend a face-off in their own zone.

Oak River won the face-off, but Elmwood's left winger blocked Jerry's pass, lifting the puck into a blooper shot. Mark saw it and swung his stick to clear it from the Otters' cage. The black rubber touched ice, bounced as it lifted on the air from Mark's blade, and rolled into his own net!

Orange arms flung up in joyful surprise.

Chug, equally surprised, snarled, "C'mon guys. I don't want to defend the net against my own team!"

Mark skated to the gate to bench himself. But Coach Evans shouted, "Get out there and play hockey!"

Brad patted Mark's red-padded backside with his hockey stick. But Mark's clenched jaw told Brad that even intended friendliness was galling.

Mark never took his eyes off the puck, driving hard for two good shots on goal, and a third—straight, fast, and accurate. It whizzed past the Elmwood goalie, not two inches from his left ear.

The cheering from Oak River's bleachers drowned the whistle for the end of the game. The team pounded Mark for avenging the goal he'd given them.

But the coach didn't see it that way. After he'd shut the dressing room door he exploded: "Never, never, never wait for action to come to you! Always, always, always go after it! Never wait for a blooper shot to land! *Bring it down with your hand!*"

Every boy bent over his skates, whipping out laces. Each knew, without looking up, who the coach was glowering at. And each knew the coach could just as easily have chewed out any of them. All were guilty of scrimmaging around a lesser team.

"And another thing . . ." Evans went through a play-by-play rerun. "Stop making every play a one-man breakaway. This is all-star hockey! That's just what it means! *All* stars, no *superstars!*

"You won the game," Coach Evans concluded. "But you played lousy. Practice at 5 P.M. in our home rink." Coach ignored the low groan that filled the dressing room. "You've got a lot of lousy play to work out of your systems, or else you'll lose tomorrow!"

Brad heard the coach's words as he stuffed his soggy pads and socks into his bag. But he was thinking about the mystery of the missing money. A kid didn't have much chance of finding anything hours after the Ontario Provincial Police and the arena management had gone through the arena.

But Brad had to try. It wasn't just this thing between him and Gary. Suspicion was showing up here in the dressing room too. Gone was the usual dumping of hockey bags out on the floor. Today they'd unpacked item by item.

Gone was the team's burst of fun-talk. Some glanced into the bags of the teammate next to them on the benches, then quickly looked away. Others joked about it as Mark did: "Hey Kurt, you're too neat not to be hiding something in that big leather bag."

Ridiculous as it sounded, suspicion had even shown up on the ice. It had been evident in the occasional hesitation before a player passed the puck—or in their not passing it at all. That is what had riled Coach Evans into calling this extra practice.

Yeah, Brad had to try to find the stolen money. He jolted

his shoulders up and down a couple of times to shake the feeling of still wearing equipment. Then, grabbing his bag, he headed for the dressing room door.

Mark was right behind him. "I'm getting out of here too." He pointed to a black-haired, tight-muscled boy, who was talking to a girl at the lunch counter. The girl looked enough like him to be his twin. "There they are."

"Hi, Cuz," the boy called to Mark. "That was pretty good— a goal in your own net and one in Elmwood's."

Mark ignored that. "Brad, meet my cousins, Steve and Bea Jaleski. Bea is short for Beatrice."

Bea threw Mark a piece of bubble gum, which he caught, unwrapped, and popped into his mouth. "You owe the till two cents," she told him.

Brad judged Steve to be the kind of kid he'd hate to meet on the ice in a tight game.

"Aren't you the defenseman who fanned on the slap shot yesterday?" Steve asked Brad.

Brad felt his stomach curl up, but he kept quiet.

"Too bad," Steve added. "I was hoping you guys would put Thunderland out. I'd love a crack at Cuz's team in the tournament. He scores for the opposition. Might as well keep it in the family, eh Mark?"

Brad saw the hangdog look on his teammate's face and knew the feeling. "Mark'll get today's goof back, 10 times over, with a team that really counts," he said. "And I'll get back that fanned shot too—maybe when we meet Thunderland in the Grand Championship."

Bea waited on a late customer while the fellows continued to talk.

"You'll get to Thunderland, only if Thunderland gets by us this afternoon," Steve reminded.

"Do us a favor, Cuz," Mark asked, "if you can't beat the team, take out their #11. We owe him one!"

"Now, Cuz," Steve scolded in mock seriousness, "is that good sportsmanship?"

"Got your money back yet?" Brad interrupted.

"Nope."

"What's the word on it?"

Steve shrugged. "Dad and I went over this place inch by inch last night. It's not hidden on any ledge or box or table or chair. We emptied every box of souvenirs and shook out every program. All we found was about $3 in loose change."

"Do you think the money is still in the arena?" Brad asked.

"Until we get our hands on it, it's anybody's guess!"

"Flip says adults like to rip off kids," Mark suggested.

"How well I know," Bea said as she returned to visit. "But this is arena-owned money. And who owns the arena? The taxpayers. The adults who were here yesterday."

"So that leaves kids who were here," Brad thought aloud.

"Why would a hockey-playing kid rip off arena money?" Steve asked. "Crumb! Some kids hang around here and work for nothing except the hockey know-how they pick up."

"Not all kids are hockey freaks, like you guys," Bea said.

"True," her brother agreed. "But then they wouldn't be hanging around an arena at Christmas break either."

But Brad knew one kid who was, and hated every minute of it.

"So what are your vibes telling you?" Mark asked.

Steve hip-checked his cousin into the wall. "Go ahead and laugh, but working in a spot like this you get a feeling about people. You get to know the ones you have to watch or you'll find something missing. You can tell who's hungry, or who's trying to get you away from the counter so he can steal something when your back is turned."

Brad got the feeling that Steve knew what he was talking about.

"Then there are the ones who have problems and don't even

see you. Don't count their change. Or walk away without it."

"You're kidding." Mark said.

"You might not believe this," Steve continued, "but some people do have problems bigger than money. There's one right there!"

Brad swung around, expecting to see Gary crutch-walking toward them. But his brother still stood by the trophy case, his full-muscled shoulders hunched over his crutches and his back half-turned to the milling crowd.

It was Oak River's #5 who was walking toward the lunch counter fully dressed, hair combed, and his equipment neatly bagged. Kurt nodded to his teammates and turned to Bea to order a hamburger, fries, and a pint of chocolate milk.

As Brad and Mark walked with Steve toward the Beaver Ridge dressing room, Mark said, "If I ate like that between meals, I'd be twice the size I am now—and it wouldn't be muscle!"

"Not if you'd run a mile, carrying a hockey bag and played a tournament game before breakfast, like he did," Steve explained.

"When Dad and I came to open the arena at 7 this morning, Kurt was jogging this way, with his hockey bag on his back. We gave him a lift. He said he'd spent the night at Beaver Lodge Motel. Their dining room is only open on weekends this time of year."

"No wonder the kid carries over $100 on him," Brad said.

"Yeah," Mark agreed. "If I'd stolen that money, I'd be afraid to go home too."

Both Mark and Brad took a second look at Kurt, who was the least known member of their team. He showed up at games and practices. His skating was OK, but he shied from checking. The coach was always screaming at him to take his man out of play.

"That kid's too well organized to be a sneak thief," Steve

said. "If he had to steal to make it to the Christmas tournament, he'd have done it a couple of weeks ago, somewhere else."

Just then they heard a shout from the hallway and saw the bread boy march in with a box of hamburger rolls held high over his shoulders.

"You're late, Westbrook," Steve called. "Can't hack the pace?"

Robby Westbrook rattled the padlock on the trophy case in passing. "Yesterday's robbery got you guys running scared? Or are these Oak River rats a threat to your silver cups?" He glowered at Gary as he spoke.

"The trophy case is always locked," Steve said. "There's always someone slinking around who likes to rip off the trophies. Some of those old loving cups on the top shelf were won by local boys who are famous now.

"But it's cash we're missing since a clumsy bread boy barged through here yesterday."

"Clumsiness, true. But not mine!" Robby Westbrook scowled at Gary before ducking into the storeroom near the lunch counter.

"Speaking of people who slink around," Steve said slowly, as he turned to look at Gary. "That kid's been hanging around here two days. He doesn't watch the games, never cheers, and doesn't buy food. He just hangs there on his crutches, staring at nothing—unless it's the trophy case."

Steve's words hit Brad like a body check into the boards. Of course Steve had no way of knowing the boy on crutches was his brother.

So all of Brad's sleuthing led nowhere—unless right back to his brother!

8

 The Kid from Acorn Creek

Brad heaved his hockey bag into the back of the station wagon before sliding into the front seat.

"That was one big win!" Mom said. "Twelve to one."

"Coach Evans didn't think so!" Brad said.

"Tired?" she asked.

Brad nodded, as he thrust his weary shoulders back, bracing himself for the usual barrage of complaints from his brother. Mom had the motor and heater fan running. Jumbo-sized snowflakes leaped and danced before the sweeping windshield wipers.

"If this keeps up, you'll have to use the snow blower again after supper so I can get the car up the driveway after work."

Gary shifted his back and craned his neck to see around the car stopped ahead of them in the 'Out" lane. "Some dumb driver's holding up the works." He slumped back. "It's that blue Corvette that brings the fancy skater on your team."

"Pete?" Brad reached for the door handle. "Is his mom stuck?"

"What do you think you can do?" Gary demanded.

Brad ignored his brother. He jumped from the car and

shuffled through the loose snow around the bumper-to-bumper vehicles waiting to get out of the parking lot.

A skier Brad had never seen before was saying with a French accent, "Madam, you will pardon my saying so, but you do not handle this machine very well. This is no dog of a car, Madam. It is just a big kitten. May I help?" He folded his 6'6" into the low-slung car.

Other would-be helpers stepped back, as none of them drove a car like this fire-red sports car, standing in the 'Enter' lane of traffic.

He drove the Peters' car onto the snowplowed shoulder of the highway without so much as one spin from its tires. "Just like I say, Madam," he called back to Julia Peters in the crowd. "She purrs just like a big kitten."

Brad got back into their car, and slowly the exit lane cleared. Cars from Maple Creek turned east while Oak River fans headed west toward Georgian Sound.

"Hey!" Brad turned in his seat as his mother stopped. Both recognized the boy propped against the steel post of a bus-stop sign poking out of the snowbank.

Brad opened the door. "Hey, Kurt! You need a ride? We're passing your place. This isn't the Lincoln Continental I've seen in your driveway, but its warmer than sitting on that snowbank."

Kurt looked in and asked permission before tossing in his hockey bag.

"You should have called us, if you needed a ride," Mom said.

Gary groaned in mock agony over her 'hockey mother' attitude. But his mother never let on she heard him. Brad had the feeling she was beginning to enjoy this tournament in spite of the extra driving and all.

"Thanks," Kurt added. "I had everything under control till the coach called the extra practice for this afternoon."

Suddenly Brad was glad they'd given Kurt a ride. Not that

he was one of his buddies. He hated playing the same shift with him because he'd never check unless the opposition hit him first. But right now he was glad to have Kurt along because he was someone to listen to besides Gary. And talking to Kurt would help Brad forget his concern over the stolen money.

Brad's mother was saying, "Your hockey is improving, Kurt. You made some good moves toward the end of the third period." She was talking as if she knew a lot about the game.

For a minute Brad wondered if his mother knew a lot more than she seemed to about other things that went on at the arena. Like Gary's standing in the hall near the front counter. And the missing money.

She talked freely to the boys, but never took her eyes from the center yellow line that periodically disappeared in the whirling white flakes. Kurt talked to her as if she were an old friend.

"I'm glad you can see some improvement," he said. "I skate and practice every chance I get, but with the creek not frozen solid yet, and the arenas booked with tournaments, it's not that much. You see, I haven't been on ice for the past two years."

"You mean you haven't skated at all in the last two years? And you made the all-star team?" Brad gulped down his surprise.

"Just barely," Kurt said.

"Crumb!" Brad forgot his annoyance at #5. "You must have really been good before."

Brad hadn't thought much about Kurt before. He knew Kurt came from the big, new house on Acorn Creek, had first-class equipment, and always had money in his pocket. But Kurt usually went his own way—a "loner," as Steve said.

"We lived in Brazil the last couple of years," Kurt revealed. "Dad is an engineer. He wants me to go to high school in

Ontario, then go on to the University of Toronto. That's why he took an engineering contract at the Olympic City in Quebec."

"Dyn-O-mite!" Brad exclaimed. "You never said anything about that before."

"You never asked."

"Have you brothers or sisters?" Mom asked.

"No. I'm afraid I'm my dad's only hope for a son in engineering."

"It must be lonely for your mother. Does she have friends or relatives in this area?"

"Not really."

"Then bring her to the hockey games," Gary said, sneering. "The arena is do-it-yourself therapy—a way to keep the family together. She should try it—it's guaranteed good for what ails you."

Kurt's jaw stiffened as he turned to look at Gary with a what-do-you-mean-by-that-crack look. He spoke slowly, in a British school accent, "Such a general statement isn't always good advice for a particular person."

Gary sputtered as if someone had kicked his crutch out from under him. "Those are my doctor's orders, and I happen to disagree with him 100%. It's the same at the arena as anywhere else for a cripple. I'm treated like an imbecile."

Kurt laughed.

Brad had never heard anyone laugh at Gary's angry complaints before.

Ruth Phillips drove at a steady 45 to 50 miles an hour, peering into the swirling snow.

Kurt swallowed his laughter and said, "I know what you mean."

"How could you know how I feel?" Gary demanded. "You're dressed like something in the Christmas windows of Eatons Center—the leather look. Look at me? For me, the only leather is in the patches to keep my crutches from wearing holes in my clothes.

"You with your air-conditioned Lincoln and your jet travel family, what do you know of my crutches-kind of living?"

Brad felt embarrassed at his brother's outburst—not for himself, he'd heard them before. But for Kurt, a courteous, soft-spoken kid, not given to enough violence to give a good body check.

"I do know how you feel! You want to scream, *'I'm not dumb!* I know what a door is for! Go away and leave me alone. I'm not a baby!'" Kurt was showing a kind of toughness Brad hadn't seen in him before.

"These past few months I've wanted to shout, 'I'm 13-years-old,'" Kurt went on. "'I can read. I've been reading since I was six. I learned the Canada food rules when I was seven. I can read a cookbook in two languages, and turn on an electric stove. I can pour a glass of milk without spilling it. I'm not an uncoordinated idiot!'" He seemed to be talking more to Mrs. Phillips in the front seat than to Gary in the back.

"It's not the little old ladies that bug me, Mrs. Phillips," Kurt continued. "It's the younger ones with brief cases and professional smiles and social workers' questionnaires. 'What did you have for dinner yesterday? How much milk do you drink? What time do you go to bed? When was the last time you had a hot meal?'"

He turned and looked directly at Gary. "I know the feeling! Everytime some Children's Aid worker gets wind that Dad's home, the worker comes out with a new bunch of forms." Kurt smiled. "This time I put a sign on the door that read, 'At the Georgian Valley Tournament.'"

"Do Annie and Ike MacTaggart still live in the farmhouse near you?" Mom asked. "How are they?"

"Ike talks tough as ever," Kurt said, "but he's getting frail. He's a good general handyman. Dad relies on him to watch our furnace and pump and that kind of thing, with him away so much. And Annie keeps house for us. She's something else! She baked all kinds of food, even though we weren't there much over Christmas. Said she couldn't bear to have such beautiful cupboards bare over Christmas."

Brad could hardly believe his ears. He'd learned more about Kurt in the half hour since he got into the car than he had in four months of school and hockey. He realized now why Kurt's efforts on the ice were rather weak. And no wonder he seemed like a loner. He *was* alone—really alone—except for the team.

And the team hadn't helped much. To the others he was just the new kid in the big house on Acorn Creek—a kid who had nicer things and more money than most of them. He didn't know as much about hockey as they did so he'd been forced to the fringe of the group.

"Was your father home for Christmas?" Mom asked.

"Only for a few hours," Kurt answered. "We spent Christmas in Toronto where we could be near Mother. She's in a hospital there."

How right Steve had been. Kurt did have a bigger problem than money!

As they crossed the Acorn Creek bridge, a bluish mist outlined a snow-wrapped, split-level house, almost lost in falling snowflakes. It reminded Brad of the loneliness he'd felt at the end of the season when he stood in the empty dressing room after his teammates had gone.

"Hey, Kurt," Brad said suddenly, "how are you going to get to practice? Why don't you stay with us now. You and I can walk over together this afternoon."

Kurt hesitated. "Well, if it's all right," he said at last.

"Of course, you're welcome," Mrs. Phillips said. "I'll be at work all afternoon, but you make yourself at home.

"And Brad, don't forget the driveway," she added.

She stopped in the road by the house since the drive was

full of snow. Brad and Kurt got out of the wagon and got their things while Gary struggled up to the house on his crutches.

Brad unlocked the kitchen door. "We'd better put some of this stuff in the dryer before practice," he told Kurt as they kicked off boots in the hall.

As he crossed the kitchen, Brad thought, *This house must seem awkward and old to Kurt.* Like the square brick plan of most of the village houses, the Phillips' had a center hallway to the front door and stairs to the basement in the main stairwell.

But Kurt was grinning at the bulletin board just inside the door. The dozen or more notes, each pinned at one corner, ruffled in the breeze from the closing door. "Looks like Big Bird's nest," he said, laughing.

Mom believes in writing things down," Brad explained. "That way we can't say we never heard her. It's right there in black and white."

After taking their things down to the dryer, Brad excused himself to go out and clean off the driveway. When he came in, he found Gary and Kurt looking over Gary's collection of model airplanes, discussing tricycle landings and tail draggers.

Near practice time, Brad and Kurt repacked their hockey bags, got into warm jackets and boots, and headed through the snow to the arena, just four blocks from the Phillips' house.

Mark hailed them across the parking lot. "Thunderland put Beaver Bridge out, 6-4," he said.

If Coach Evans needed anything to add to his annoyance with the Otters' game that day, that was it!

"OK, who's missing?" He ran an eye along the benches in the dressing room. "Pete?"

No reply.

"Maybe his mother ran off with that duded-up skier," Flip said.

"If she did, they drove off into the sunset in separate Corvettes."

"Wow!" Wouldn't that be great? A two-vet family?"

"Get with it, guys!" Coach bellowed at the boys. "It's shooting, passing, speed and more speed!"

Somehow Brad and Mark were shuffled to the end of the line as they began the drills. Brad heard the coach arguing with Joe LaBlanc, the assistant coach. "But centermen are supposed to score. Sure, Pete'll score when the team is a couple goals down. But he doesn't care about shooting most of the time. He gets more kicks out of passing!"

"Maybe he thinks like a winger," Joe said.

"But he's capable of being a *good* centerman! The way that kid can pick the spots with the puck when he wants to!" Coach Evans wasn't a coach to pick on a kid, but he was uptight about something now.

"You saw him, Joe. Nobody was passing today, except Pete, who is supposed to shoot. Why?" the coach continued. "Beats me! With the speed and reflexes of a pro, the kid acts as if he doesn't want to score!"

With a double blast from coach's whistle, 16 boys in mismatched shirts, each with his favorite NHL team, wove in and out and around pylons, and over hurdles, down on one knee, up on blades—full speed ahead. No time to think of anything except pass, shoot, check, speed, and more speed.

Only after energy drained into emptiness and muscles turned to jelly and skin stung with the salt of their own sweat—only then did the final whistle blow.

Sixteen boys flopped exhausted on benches, their padding sweat-glued to their flesh. The dressing room door opened. A policeman in a parka walked in and asked, "Is Kurt Carpenter here?"

Every exhausted gasp for air ceased as 15 pairs of eyes watched.

"Here, sir," Kurt spoke with a courtesy learned in an out-of-country, British boarding school. He followed the policeman out.

A communal breath expelled as the energy of curiosity spurred 15 boys into action.

"They called him by name! What'd they want Kurt for? Do you think . . .?"

Group imagination burst forth like hockey fans over a winning goal.

"Aw, c'mon guys," Brad spoke loud and clear. "Before practice it was Pete. Now it's Kurt. If I walk out of the room, will I be the next suspect?"

The buzz thinned out but persisted as the fellows repacked and hurried into their clothes. Andy grumbled. "I played hockey for four years at the Falls, and the police never checked our dressing rooms. But they've checked this team twice in one week—in two different arenas!"

"How do you know Kurt wasn't called to the telephone?" Brad asked.

The half dozen boys left in the dressing room laughed. "By a uniformed policeman?"

Kurt ran in, "Hey Brad, Dad's been trying to reach me by phone all day. Can I give the long distance operator your number for him to call in about half an hour?" Kurt repeated the number after Brad and dashed back to the arena office.

"Hey, guys!" Brad gloated. "It *was* a phone call and there's probably a sensible reason for Pete not making the extra practice."

"Yeah, 'cause nothing exciting ever happens to us," Mike agreed.

"So do we have to make up stories of thieves on our team to scare ourselves silly—like kids telling ghost stories?" Brad asked.

Disappointedly they agreed.

"We play Maple Creek tomorrow," Mark added. "And Hawkley Falls will probably win their game. They're no pushover either. They took the Consolation Championship last year."

Kurt and Brad walked on through the falling snow toward Brad's house. The only sound was the soft swish-swishing of their hockey bags brushing against their legs. The boys were too tired to do anything but let the weight bump against them with each step into the soft snow.

"The police said Montreal is snowbound," Kurt explained. "All transportation has stopped and the phones were tied up for hours. Dad's been trying to get me all day—at the motel and arena and the house. He was frantic—called the police."

On the top of each village streetlight sat a glistening cone of golden snowflakes. Beyond them the night was a silver-flecked midnight blue. It was difficult for the boys to believe a storm would be coming this way.

"But if the snow starts to blow—" Brad began but didn't finish. It took a few minutes for them to grasp the trouble snowbound roads could cause a tightly scheduled hockey tournament. It could mean whole teams stranded away from home. With no bread, milk, or meat deliveries, the arenas, lodges, and motels would run out of food. The kids wouldn't have enough money for extra days away.

"Wow, can you imagine what it would be like for the poor team managers and coaches?" Brad said. "The Thunderland team stays in a nearby motel. If we get snowbound, Thunderland could win by default."

"That would rile Art plenty, wouldn't it?" Kurt added.

"You know the coach?"

"Yeah. I met him at an Alteen meeting."

"A what?" Brad asked.

"Alteen. It's part of Alcoholics Anonymous, for children with a member of their family who is an alcoholic, like my mother.

Helps us understand how to cope. Did you know that Art Evans played in the National Hockey League? He says playing hockey was so easy for him that he began thinking success was easy. He started to break training to drink. Then success wasn't so easy, so he drank more. He suggested to Dad that I try out for the team. I know I have to work twice as hard as you fellows, but it's great being part of a group."

Brad felt his face grow hot under the cold touch of snow-flakes, ashamed of his part in shuffling #5 to the fringes of dressing room gossip. He changed the subject by saying, "With a storm coming this way, who knows when your dad's call will come through. You might as well stay the night. We're due back at Beaver Bridge at 9 o'clock tomorrow morning."

"I'd hate to be halfway between houses when Dad called. Would your mother mind?"

"Nope. Mom likes people. Even Gary doesn't seem to mind you. And he hasn't liked anybody since the accident. Not even himself."

"*Especially* himself," Kurt said. "That's Alteen talking. I've heard Dad say it to Mother hundreds of times. 'Evelyn, Evelyn you don't have to perform to be liked. You just have to be honest.' "

"I know what you mean," Brad said. He was thinking more of Gary than Kurt—of Gary and his idea that a paraplegic didn't fit into "normal" crowds.

"Dyn-O-mite! Am I hungry!" Brad said, changing the subject again.

The boys shuffled along faster, stirring up snow clouds at their feet.

9

 # Kurt Asks
the Right Questions

The third tournament game, the Maple Creek match, was one game Coach Evans liked. He strutted up and down, rocking from heel to toe. "Good work!" he congratulated. "You played a great game! It was a well-earned win. 4-2 is a good score! Some of you will make hockey players yet—with a little luck and a lot more sweat!

"Now speed it up! Hawkley Falls is next, and they're fast. If you play like you played today, only double time, we could squeak a win out of their team and take the consolation trophy."

Brad felt a groan inside where no one heard. He had so much yet to learn about hockey. Until this Georgian Valley Tournament, hockey was speed and accuracy, weariness and joy. Somewhere in the thrill of laying wood on rubber and hearing the fans in the bleachers burst with cheers, there was something he'd missed.

Winning wasn't enough. It was *who* you defeated and *where* on the schedule. Mark and Steve talked about it after the Beaver Bridge team was put out by Thunderland in their third game.

"If we'd lost our first game to Thunderland like you Otters, instead of our third, we'd still be in the tournament. We'd be playing our way down the losing side like you—taking the easy way to the championship games," Steve said.

It had been agreed that Kurt would spend the night with them. Ruth Phillips called Annie MacTaggart, Kurt's housekeeper, to tell her Kurt would be staying with them. She assured Annie that Kurt had talked with his father and was welcome to stay with them until the tournament was over, or as long as the Otters were winning.

"I didn't realize how little other boys come around our place now," Ruth Phillips told Kurt. "They used to be in and out all the time before the accident. So welcome to our home, Kurt."

Kurt looked at her with the sidewise smile of a serious boy. In the house he talked more with Gary than Brad and often on topics Brad knew nothing about.

Since Gary's accident, Brad had surpassed his older brother physically. As Gary talked to Kurt about airplanes and oil wells, bridges and Brazil, Brad realized that his brother had been growing in other ways.

When Brad came up from his shower that night, Kurt was already in the other bed in the room Brad had shared with Gary before the accident. Now Gary had a wide double bed in the spare room.

From force of habit, Brad took out his Bible and notebook. He felt Kurt watching and looked up.

"You and your brother are so different," Kurt said.

"What do you mean?" Brad asked.

"You pray. Why?" Kurt asked.

"I believe the Lord hears me when I pray."

"What makes you think that the things you pray about don't come by coincidence?"

"Well—I guess it's because of the way I *feel after* I've

prayed in addition to what God's Word says," Brad explained.

Kurt lay on his back, with his hands under his head, staring at the ceiling. "I suppose the South American Indian feels something too when he prays. The Quechua Indian leaves little stick messages on the trails for help from the spirits. Dad said he wasn't sure whether it was to inform God of their affairs or to misinform the devil."

When Brad said nothing, Kurt went on.

"I've been in church services where the prayers left me with the same feeling. A kind of snow job. Who needs prayer? If God is God, who needs to tell Him anything. Like a kid telling tales to his mother about someone who's wronged him, and mother already knows more about the right and wrong than the tattler does. So?"

Brad explained how he felt about his prayer talk sessions with the Lord Jesus after he'd made the team at the arena and had come home to the hassle over hockey in the family.

"I opened my Bible that night and read the Lord's prayer in Matthew 6:6-15. When I came to the part about forgiving those who sin against you, I realized I had to forgive a lot of people. I felt people had wronged me with all their pat-on-the-head sayings about feeling sorry for my brother and being grateful it wasn't me. They made me want to scream, 'I *am* grateful, but I still want to play hockey!'

"It was the prayer 'lead me not into temptation but deliver me from evil' that cut me loose. I'm still praying that the Lord will keep me from resenting Gary."

"Hmmm," Kurt said. "Then your kind of praying isn't to clue God in but to clue yourself in!"

"Yeah, that's it," Brad agreed. "It was the next day the doctor suggested the tournament as a normal family activity."

Kurt grinned. "And now I'm part of that 'back to normal' life."

"And if we take Hawkley Falls tomorrow, we've got a consolation championship!" Brad said. "And a chance to play Grand Championship. Wow!"

"Hmm." Kurt's mutter was an agreeable, sleepy sound.

10

 Navies vs. Reds

Next morning as Brad and Kurt pulled their equipment from the car, icy bits of snow swirled over them, gusting down from the Beaver Bridge arena roof.

Brad wiped his face with his coat sleeve. "As my great-grandfather, the sea captain, used to say, 'A wind from the East is fit for neither man nor beast.'" He waved his right hand, with two hockey sticks in it, to Steve who lifted his broom from the last sweep of the sidewalks.

Robby Westbrook dashed for the doorway ahead of them. "Couldn't hack the pace with Thunderland either?" He sneered at Steve, as he stomped two bootloads of snow onto the swept walk.

"At least we made the team, Westbrook." Steve recleaned the pavement in three swipes. "Don't clump half the parking lot into the arena. Wet floors can be dangerous. You should know that by now!"

As Brad followed Steve through the doorway, he asked, "What's he got against you?"

"Robby? Oh he mean-mouths everybody. At least all the kids on the Beaver Bridge all-star team. He works vacations on his dad's bread route, so this is his week to pester us."

"Won't his dad let him play hockey?" Brad asked.

"Nah, it's not that. The crazy kid can skate as well as half our team. But at tryouts he kept cheating in the races and cutting corners on drills. He slouched when he thought the trainers weren't looking and poured it on when he thought they were. The coaches dropped him on the second cut."

Cheers from the bleachers rocked the arena as Glengarry scored on Thunderland. "That makes it a 3-3 tie," Steve said. "That'll put Pop in a bad humor for the morning. It's the overtimes that ruin his scheduling."

A group of blue-jacketed boys came through the double swinging doors from the bleachers. Steve explained to the Oak River players. "After the bruising Thunderland gave us yesterday, our team is here to cheer against them."

"Oh-oh," Steve said to Mark. "Here come the cops again."

Two uniformed men strolled down the hall. Dressed in heavy police boots and thick parkas they ambled like a pair of mean-looking bears.

"Still looking around here?" Brad asked.

"They come in for coffee every time Thunderland or Oak River play. And Bea's coffee's not that good!" Steve said.

As they passed the boys, Brad heard one say, "That crippled kid must have everything memorized by now."

Brad's breath froze in his throat. Did they suspect Gary?

Steve was watching, puzzled. "I can't see why they're interested in him. He gives off the wrong vibes to be real trouble. Pretends he's not interested, but I bet he can add things up."

Knowing how sour his brother was at times, Brad wondered if Gary's addition would get the right answers.

"Maybe they think he sees something they don't," Mark added.

"Maybe it's just that a handicapped kid is always noticed

in a crowd," Kurt suggested, "easily remembered as an Oak River fan."

Just then the hall emptied of fans as Thunderland and Glengarry went back to the ice to play out their sudden death overtime. Meanwhile, the Oak River and Hawkley Falls teams headed for separate dressing rooms to get ready for their match.

As Brad flashed around the rink with his team in their stretching and loosening exercises, he realized this game was all that stood between Oak River and another chance at Thunderland. If they won today, they'd play tomorrow to decide the grand champion.

The Oak River cheering section had doubled in the four days of play. But Hawkley Falls, like Thunderland, had stayed in a motel nearby because their hometown was so far away. The few fans that showed up to cheer for them didn't give a true showing of parent interest or team enthusiasm.

Coach Evans walked up and down behind the bench as the players circled the rink. "Play it tight! Their wingers are fury on ice! Look where you pass. You'll have to block them at the blue line. Don't let them wind up. Check! Check! You hear me, Kurt! Check 'em at the blue line or you've lost 'em!

"You forwards . . . score! Never mind any fancy play in their zone. You're out there to score! You hear me, Pete? Score!"

Coach Evans' instructions rang in their ears—Block 'em at the blue line!

"Hey, Turkey," Mark called. "It's you and me at the blue line."

The Hawkley Falls team stalked onto the ice. None of the 17 players were as big as either Mark or Brad, but they looked good in yellow helmets and navy shirts with yellow trim. They looked strong on their feet—and fast!

After three minutes of play, the Otters knew these boys in the navy shirts could play the angles. They sliced, jabbed, and fancy-stepped the puck away from Oak River. But Flip and Jerry drove hard, pushing for an opening. The defense worked their line. And six minutes into play, each team had only one good shot on goal.

As lines changed, Coach Evans patted each player coming off the ice. "Keep it up boys. You're playing great! You've got them figured out. Now score!"

During one change, Mark was on defense with Don. When Jerry was cornered by Hawkley Falls #6 and #12, he froze the puck for a face-off.

Katie Maloney shouted something about illegal play going on against the boards. By the look on her face, it wasn't Sunday School language.

Jerry shook his head, gulped air, and nodded.

Katie screamed, "Hey you zebra-shirts, you're supposed to watch the action *after* the whistle too! There's a hospital just a mile away. Why don't you refs hurry over and get a brain transplant."

The few Hawkley Falls fans, across the rink, made their share of noise. They booed when play stopped at the Otters' blue line. And the Oak River boosters cheered when play reversed to the Hawkley Falls zone.

Every scoreless minute of play caused each team to try harder. Brad felt his skin oozing sweat under his pads, and his hairline trickling the salty water onto his face.

"You're playing great, guys!" Coach Evans told the line change. He laid a hand on Kurt and added seriously, "You've got to check, boy. Twice you let them through. Pete's speed and Chug's goalie glove were all that stopped them from scoring. This game is for the consolation championship! This is all that stands between us and a chance at the grand championship title!"

Kurt nodded agreeably.

"Look, lad," Coach crouched to glower at Kurt, eyeball to

eyeball, "you don't get it, do you? What I'm saying is, there's something worse than losing this game. That's leaving your defense partner wide open for a two-man attack. Defensemen must defend each other too!"

By halftime Oak River's players welcomed the chance to catch their breath. The speed of this Hawkley team was a pressure they hadn't played against before. Hawkley Falls wasn't mean in the corners, like some, but if the Otters didn't play all-out, the Navy shirts moved one stride ahead of them at every turn.

Now the fans were turning on them! Katie Maloney promised Jerry all sorts of murder and mayhem if he didn't get a goal.

Pete nudged Brad on the bench. "Mother doesn't go for this hockey mother stuff."

This surprised Brad, for Pete's mother was always there, dressed to enjoy the games. She attended the practices too, except for the extra one the Coach had called yesterday.

Then he noticed what Pete meant. Julia Peters and Ruth Phillips had shifted as far from Katie's cowbell as possible.

The whistle sounded to end the second period. At time-out, between the second and third period, when the ice machine cleared the ice surface, Coach Evans took Pete aside. "Stop playing ring-around-a-rosey! This isn't Elmwood you're playing now. You're playing for a championship."

The coach split Brad and Mark and sent Kurt out with Brad to begin the third period.

Brad played steady, working his line, but managed only two shots on goal: one wide and the other palmed by their goalie.

As the minutes flicked by on the electric numbers, each shift began to look like a replay of the one before. Every shift in the Oak River pattern of play brought a successful countershift from the Hawkley team. And vice versa.

At nine minutes into the third period, it was still a 0-0 game. No championship game was a tie. They had to play until somebody scored.

The longer the game went on, the wearier the players became. And the stronger the gut-urge Brad felt to score. He promised himself that at the first sight of the puck, he'd slap one on. The hunger to score tightened every nerve in his body.

Skating out from a rest shift, Brad's desire to score gave fresh strength to his legs, his arms, and his hands.

The puck dropped, Pete scooped it to Brad who pulled in the pass and slammed it up the boards to Flip.

"Shoot!" Coach Evans bellowed as Pete picked it off the boards inside the blue line. Slap! Their goalie palmed it, and dropped it to the ice.

The Otter fans groaned. The coach let out a sound like a wounded animal as play moved the full length of the ice before being whistled down for an offside.

Brad felt his hopes quicken as the ref moved for a face-off just outside the Hawkley zone. He held his stick down, his head up, and his body in a lunge position ready for the drop.

Pete scooped the face-off to Kurt who was crouched on the right end of the blue line. The Hawkley wingers drove for the puck, but Kurt passed it through his attackers. Brad, left in the clear, met the puck outside the slot.

Slam! A ripple of feeling ran up his arm. Noisy cheers burst out like the booming of spring ice breakup in the bay, pounding giant ice slabs onto the shale shore. Only the pounding was on him. His teammates danced on their blades, arms flung upward, their sticks high. They pommelled him on every side. Their shouts exploded in his ears.

"We scored! We scored! We scored!"

Brad felt a tiny bubble of silence inside. A strange quietness in the tumult of cheering. That Friend that sticks closer than a brother. And joy like a roaring waterfall all around him.

As he skated out from his rest shift, Brad noticed the electric digits read 3 minutes and 11 seconds to go. And the score still stood, Oak River 1, Hawkley Falls 0.

Again Pete took the face-off. He backpassed to Kurt. Again two navy men moved right on the blue line. Only this time they lunged at the man without even trying for the puck. Brad kept the puck from slithering into the neutral zone, then lifted his stick to shoot. Suddenly he was spun around by a charge from behind, his stick still in midair.

Oak River fans screamed for a penalty.

Kurt went down after being pinned to the boards by two Hawkley Falls players.

Brad heard the whistle, but he was all that stood between Kurt and two angry Hawkley defensemen. He didn't know whether it was the Otters or Hawkley Falls the fans were hurling abusive threats at, but he wasn't about to back off to find out.

A second whistle blast brought both striped-shirt officials into the scuffle. Kurt folded himself together to rise, took a gasp of air, and buckled.

Brad knew the feeling of getting the wind knocked out and gasping for air to ease the burning, only to have the oxygen burn all the hotter in your lungs.

On his second try, Kurt stood up slowly and skated with shoulders drooping to the bench. Brad skated alongside him.

The PA blared: Oak River penalties: #5, Carpenter, 2 minutes for cross-checking; #4, Phillips, 2 minutes for high-sticking.

Kurt cross-checking? [17] Brad couldn't believe his ears on that. Anymore than he could believe his high-sticking [18] call. Sure his stick was in the air! He'd been swung around by a Hawkley Falls player.

---

[17] *Cross-checking* is given a two-minute penalty. It's using the shaft of the stick across the body of an opponent, usually with two hands on the stick.
[18] When a player lifts a stick off the ice in a defensive move against another player it's called *high-sticking*. It usually results in a two-minute penalty.

The cheers turned angry. Fans from both sides of the ice threatened the referees. Oak River bombarded them with charges of bad calls while Hawkley Falls ordered the refs not to change the calls.

Brad plunked down on the bench in the penalty box next to Kurt. "What happened?" he asked.

"I guess my stick was across him, all right," Kurt said. "He had his shoulder in my gut, holding me against the boards. I didn't think you could do that when the puck had been passed."

"You can't, if the ref sees it!" Brad said glumly. He prepared to agonize through the next two minutes of helplessness and prayed that the team could hold their one-goal lead! He'd seen more experienced teams than the Otters lose a one-goal advantage with two players in the penalty box. The unfairness of it all was an agony inside him.

In spite of Katie Maloney's "What are they paying you, ref?" the game went on.

Hawkley Falls won the face-off and drove for the Otters' net with nothing but open ice between!

Not an Otter defenseman was on the ice! What was Coach Evans thinking of? Oak River was wide open for defeat! Brad tasted tears inside his mouth.

He was afraid to look!

A rumbling of "ohs" arose, but no cheers. No goal?

Brad looked up, saw Pete check Hawkley #12 off a chance to shoot, then pass the puck back to Flip. Flip passed to Jerry. And Jerry back to Pete. And they did it *again! And again!*

Placed like three points on an imaginary triangle, the three Oak River forwards passed the puck from one to the other. Everytime a Hawkley player moved toward the puck that Otter passed to another point of the triangle.

After a few second of stunned silence in the bleachers, a few guffaws broke into a ripple of laugher.

Flip to Jerry, Jerry to Pete. Caught on the left by a Hawkley man, Pete passed right to Jerry.

The Falls coach, with the shoulders of a prize fighter and the voice of a hog caller, leaned far over the boards screaming a stream of threats at his rattled boys.

Some of the younger brothers of the Otters' players started to chant, "Ring-around-a-rosey, a pocket full of posies."

Coach Evans strutted up and down behind the bench, rocking from heel to toe, chuckling, "Go to it, Pete. You wanted to play ring-around-a-rosey, go to it!"

The five navies were scrambling around and across the red-shirted triangle, trying to steal the puck. But always the Oak River-three passed a split second too soon to be caught in a two-on-one squeeze.

The Hawkley Falls coach shouted himself hoarse, calling out what he'd do when he got his hands on his team to pound some sense into them. Finally he threw up his hands in disgust.

What good was a two-man advantage, if Hawkley Falls never got control of the puck?

"Keep it up! Keep it up! Keep it up!" the Oak River fans chanted.

Even some of the Hawkley Falls parents smiled, and shook their heads.

It was the longest two minutes of gametime ever played by the Oak River team. Not one whistle was blown—not one Otter was checked. And the three controlled the puck through the whole double penalty.

With 48 seconds left in the game, the Otters had their team back. They'd killed the double penalty! They still had their one-goal lead!

After the humiliating scramble around the red triangle, Hawkley Falls played it cagey—one man to one man—no more two-man rushes.

Coach Evans sent out his penalty-killing string, but five men strong this time, with Mark and Brad on defense, Jerry, Flip, and Pete playing up. His orders: "Control the puck! Kill time!"

Fans shouted orders and screamed threats, with the volume of noise equal from either side.

With 10 seconds left in the game, the Oak River fans started the countdown: "Ten, nine, eight . . ."

Brad could hardly believe his ears, but he didn't dare take his eyes off the play to check.

"Seven, six, five." The chanters were pushing a half second ahead of the digital clock.

"Four, three, two . . ."

"One!"

We won! We won! *We won!*

The final whistle blew. Cowbells clanged. Gloves flew off. Red helmets rolled on the ice.

The Otters hugged and pounded each other, shouting, "We did it! We did it!"

The Oak River Otters, the unknowns in tournament play!

The Otters, winning their way down the losing side, had made it! They had won the consolation championship!

"We made it to the grand championship game!" they cheered.

"Dyn-O-mite!"

"Thunderland, here we come!"

11

 Thunderland, Here We Come!

Shouts of, "We won! We won!" rang from the rafters as the Oak River players lined up along one of the blue lines and the Hawkley Falls along the other.

Mark, as captain of the Otters, skated out to center circle, received the broad-based, silver cup from Jake Jaleski, the tournament host, and shook hands. Then he skated the full circle of the ice surface, with the team behind him in a follow-the-leader line.

Fans cheered their win all over again. A consolation championship for a new tournament team was quite an accomplishment!

Photo bulbs flashed. The CKGV newsman made notes as the TV cameras whirred.

And the Oak River Otters couldn't quite believe this heady feeling of having won their way down the losing side to become consolation champions of the Georgian Valley Tournament.

As the teams shook hands, the Hawkley Falls players walked past, glum-faced and sullen. Some offered a limp hand. Some put their hands behind their backs and refused to look at the winners. Several said, "Good luck with Thunderland." One said, "That turkey on your team is a chicken!" And he went off clucking like a hen.

Oak River fans waited to congratulate their boys as they made their way to the dressing room.

"Good game! Well done! Great penalty killing!"

Good penalty killing, Brad thought, *but a bad penalty*.

Brad's Mom and Julia Peters were with the other happy Otter families. But Gary wasn't celebrating. He made his way awkwardly through the crowd and away from them.

Once in the dressing room, Coach Evans said, "You played a great game! It was a well-deserved win!"

He gave them about three minutes to sag on the benches before he said, "Now, about tomorrow—"

While the boys enjoyed the drinks and hot dogs sent in by their proud parents, Coach laid it on the line.

"Tomorrow's the grand championship game against a two-time champion. Thunderland has the strongest team. Anyway they cut their lines, you'll have six tough players to face all the time!

"But," Evans bellowed, "they're at a disadvantage. They *think* they can take you! They put you out once. Now it's up to you to show them they can't do it a second time!"

Brad felt the excitment of winning turn to jelly in his joints. All the energy oozed out of him.

On the way home, the words "It's up to you" echoed in his head. He sat in the car too tired to talk.

"How do you feel, Kurt?" Mrs. Phillips asked.

"Got the wind knocked out of me, that's all. It hurt at the time, but I'm OK now. Just imagine, a consolation championship! I can't believe it! I can hardly wait to tell Dad. And boy, will he find it hard to believe too!"

"And you, Brad?" Mom asked. "You weren't as excited about the win as some of the boys."

Brad didn't catch the concern in his mother's voice.

"Yeah. I got caught with my stick up like a beginner, then came to Kurt's defense too late!" Brad sighed but it came out a sob. For a second he thought he was going to cry—cry like a baby.

"Brad! This is *your* mother you're talking to. Not some hockey mother who expects a superman performance every second of play. That's not life."

"Yeah, Brad!" Kurt exclaimed. "We *won* the game!"

"Right," Gary said grudgingly. "And you scored the winning goal!"

"Hey, man, that's right!" Brad elbowed Kurt beside him. "It *was* the winning goal. It was the only goal! Decent!"

"It was a beauty!" Kurt agreed. "I wish I could put them away like that."

"You will, with practice." *Wow!* Brad thought to himself. *How crazy mixed-up a guy can get when he picks up resentment!* He'd resented being caught out and not getting to Kurt in time; being held down by a Hawkley player from a good slap shot; and the penalty.

Mixed-up was right. He'd felt as if he'd lost rather than won. Slowly, the tightness inside him unwound and he said it again, "We won. We really did! Boy, we couldn't have squeaked by Hawkley Falls on any less, could we? A 1-0 game!"

"You'll probably be on tonight's TV news," Kurt added. "You'll be the Oak River success story."

Gary's voice lacked the I-told-you-so stab when he said, "Matt, the CKGV newsman, says *I'm* a success story. He says that being able to walk with crutches after having a broken back is a success. I'd never thought of that angle before."

"I saw him taking pictures of you," Mom said. "Didn't you mind?"

"Sure I minded!" Gary said. "But this Matt character says

what he means, instead of stumbling around, afraid the wrong words might jump out."

"Is he laughing at hockey?" Mom asked.

"Not the game," Gary said. "Just the way people act at it. When Brad scored, he caught Katie Maloney three feet off the bench, arms swinging and mouth wide open. She was clanging her cowbell for all she was worth."

Although it was only noon, Mom switched on the headlights. Huge snowflakes glistened and danced in the twin beams of yellow light.

"Can we beat Thunderland tomorrow?" Kurt asked Gary.

"Maybe, if you put out championship effort." Gary rattled his crutches together. "If it weren't for these iron limbs, I'd be playing too. I'd play better than you guys. I'd never get beat on a slap shot in the last second of play or stop play for a tin whistle in the bleachers."

Both Otters turned around to look at Gary. "You *knew* there was a whistle?" They spoke at the same time.

"After the teams were off the ice," Gary began, "I saw a kid in the lobby stuffing a plastic toy in his mother's purse while she went on to a friend about how great Thunderland was.

"The kid acted as if he'd played a big joke on everyone. I followed him and his friends into the washroom to see what was so funny. A kid on crutches is nobody so he just went on gloating over the trick as if I weren't there.

"Anyway, you're the big heroes! What was I to you?" Gary continued and answered his own question. "I was someone to blame when things went wrong. I know some of you think I took the money."

"You did have a ringside seat to the action," Brad said. "And you acted mad enough to do a dumb thing like that."

"Ringside seat! I was on my ear on the floor with my crutches underneath me!"

Suddenly Brad heard the laughter in his brother's voice and thought, *He's glad I felt bad.*

"Look, you dummies," Gary was saying. "I see a lot around there, a lot you guys never notice. With nothing to do but hang around, a guy gets hunches." Gary sobered. "If you dummies can sit still long enough to listen to a cripple, I'll tell you a few things that'll help you tomorrow."

"We're listening," Kurt said.

"OK. Thunderland's #8 and #11 are their toughies. Check them everytime one of them lays a stick on the puck. If you don't take anything off them, the rest of them will settle down and play good hockey. Number 2 is their rusher. Never let him wind up. He'll score every time. If you'd read the tournament records posted in the hall you'd know he scores more than half their goals. So keep the puck away from #2 and you cut Thunderland's chances in half!"

Gary went on. "There's a couple of troublemakers among their fans, with more than toy whistles up their sleeves. I saw them heckling the Beaver Bridge boys along the boards."

"What are our chances?" Kurt asked.

"About 1 in 10."

And it wasn't a put-down. Gary meant it. Both Kurt and Brad bowed their heads in despair.

"But that's all the odds you need if you want to win badly enough. Oh, how I wish I could—" Gary didn't finish his sentence.

Brad knew this wasn't ridicule or spite or any of the other things Gary had hurled at him and his friends. This time, Brad felt his brother's honest urge to play the game. Gary's legs were dead, but the urge to use them wasn't. And somehow, knowing Gary cared made the need to win more urgent than Gary's jeering ever had.

12

 Ride Through
a Storm

The morning of the Grand Championship game dawned bright and cold. Clouds of steam churned upward from the freezing water of Oak River.

"A winter fog would freeze a dog." Another of Brad's store of sailor sayings from his great-grandfather.

"That I believe," Kurt said, shivering. "After a couple of winters in the tropics, this is hard to take."

"It's cold even to us natives!" Gary grumbled.

Ruth Phillips said nothing. She drove with both hands on the steering wheel, both eyes searching the whiteness ahead, and both ears tuned to the Canadian long-range weather report on the car radio.

Gary had dropped angry ridicule and glum silence. Instead he talked of Thunderland, its team, parents, fans, coach—everything he'd seen of them both on and off the ice.

He advised, advised, advised, until the sound of his voice grated in Brad's ears like a fresh piece of chalk on a clean chalkboard.

Brad's nerves were tightening up like the spring of a watch being wound.

Ticktock, ticktock.

"Thunderland is staying in a nearby motel," Gary said. "If you guys can't get on the ice on time, they'll win by default!"

Ticktock, ticktock, ticktock.

Ruth edged the car as close as she dared to the right wall of plowed snow to make room for the vehicle churning up the cloud of white that was rolling toward them down the middle of the road. A blur of yellow headlights zoomed past in a whiteout.

"I hope we don't meet anything wider than that!" Mrs. Phillips exclaimed. "Drifting snow has certainly narrowed this road."

Ticktock, ticktock.

"We should find the driving better when we turn due east," she said. "We'll be running parallel with the wind. We'll get there—us and the angels!"

Ticktock, ticktock, ticktock.

Six minutes and three miles farther along, Brad realized the slower his mother drove the faster the clock inside him ticked.

"Look out!" Brad yelled. A cyclone of snow whirled down the road toward them. Ruth steered right till the right car fender brushed the piled snow and the rear wheels spun in icy ruts at the edge of the road.

The cyclone seemed to gain speed and size as it rushed toward them.

A silver cylinder rumbled by with barely enough clearance to show daylight between the two vehicles.

"A bulk milk truck!" Gary said. "Likely Baysview Dairy. I should report him for careless driving in bad road conditions."

Ticktock, ticktock.

Ruth tried to ease the car out of the snowbank, but the front wheels wouldn't jump the ruts. Even a slight touch of the accelerator sent the rear wheels into a whining spin.

She tried to back out the same way she'd gotten in. Still the tires whined. They seemed to be hopelessly trapped in slots of ice.

Ticktock, ticktock, ticktock.

The doors on the right side of the car were blocked by the snowbank. Brad turned around in the seat to see what to do next. "There's a shovel and tow chain in the back." He and Kurt crawled over the seats, across their hockey bags, and out the tailgate.

"Shut the door. It's freezing in here," Gary complained.

Ticktock, ticktock.

The boys worked frantically to break down the ice ruts that trapped the tires.

Brad hacked ice with the shovel, while Kurt chainwhipped the ridges that were built up from midafternoon thawing on sunny afternoons and refreezing after sunset.

"Here comes a car," Gary shouted.

Brad ran out into the center of the road, waving his arms like a windmill in a hurricane.

Ticktock, ticktock.

The big blob of red purred to a stop. A man unfolded from a red sports car. It was the skier from the tournament parking lot.

"You're one of the Oak River boys, no?" he pointed to Brad's team jacket.

"Yes, but we're stuck. And we play in 35 minutes! Can you tow us out of here?"

"This is no tow truck I drive." He sounded horrified at the suggestion. But he folded himself low to examine the problem without getting a fleck of snow on his ski clothes.

He straightened. "As I say, this is no tow truck. But I'm one grand driver." He explained what he would do in laughing, French-accented gestures.

Gary rolled down the window and demanded, "What's he laughing at?"

He'd complain if help came with angel wings, Brad thought. *Ticktock, ticktock, ticktock.*

Just as easily as he'd pulled Pete's mother's car up the incline in the parking lot earlier in the week, the skier eased the station wagon back onto the highway.

When Ruth tried to thank him, he only laughed. "The boys! They must play hockey! Good luck in the game, boys. And good luck to you, madam." And he was gone.

"Thank you, Lord," Ruth said softly as the car moved forward again.

Brad felt nothing but the clock ticking, ticking, ticking, until the tension twisted his insides in knots.

Short prayers had become a diversion to that ticking, or else he'd be wound up too tight to be any good to the team when he did get there! *Father, thank You for getting us out of the snowbank and help us get to the arena on time.*

"Maybe the first game will go into overtime," Kurt said.

"Maybe it won't," Gary replied.

When Ruth stopped at the door of the Beaver Bridge arena to let the boys out, she flexed her fingers several times as if to assure herself they were still hers, and not permanently welded to the steering wheel.

"We're here! We're here!" the boys cheered.

The ticktock turned to a chomp-chomp-chomp of boys in winter boots running with equipment bags across the rubber matting.

Coach Evans directed them to Room 3.

One yell, 14 voices strong, rang in their ears as Brad and Kurt unzipped, snapped, and buckled on layer after layer, "Where's my sweater?" Brad looked up and noticed the whole dressing room was ready—*except for team sweaters!* Where were they?

"Mark?" he called.

"Not here yet," Flip answered. "And his dad has the sweaters."

"Oh no!" Brad groaned. Worse than no sweaters was no Mark!

The clock started ticking again.

13

 Battle for
the Trophy

What seemed like eons later, Joe LaBlanc and his son Mark came charging into the dressing room each carrying an armload of the Otters' sweaters on wire hangers.

Mark breathed a sigh of relief and explained, "Dad swerved to miss a car and wound up in a ditch. We had to call a tow truck to get us out. Boy, am I happy to see you guys!"

Then it struck the Oak River team that the scheduled starting time had passed 15 minutes before and no Beaver Bridge official had come in to tell them they'd be disqualified if they weren't on the ice. But that mystery had to wait. They had a championship game to play.

Brad was only three minutes into the game when he realized this was going to be the toughest hour of his 13-year-old life. Thunderland was playing excellent hockey. They had the edge on the Oak River team because they had played together as a team for several years.

With tight calls from the refs, and all-out action from the players, it looked as if the team with the most endurance would win this championship.

Katie Maloney had warned the boys—the first goal wins a

championship! It certainly had been true in the consolation game! The first goal scored was the only goal.

A whistle signaled an offside pass. Mark shrugged. "I'm still shaking from thinking we'd be late. Can you imagine making it to the grand championship, but getting here too late to play? The whole thing scared me silly!"

"You're here!" Brad told him. "And we're four minutes into the first period. So pull yourself together. We've got to do it now!"

In the agonizing minutes before the game when they'd waited in the dressing room for the call "teams to the ice," Coach Evans had been at his coaching best. His words still rang in Brad's ears, as the coach intended they should: "Trust yourselves. Play better than you ever played before. Let yourselves go!"

Suddenly Thunderland rushed, four abreast, up the neutral ice toward the Oak River zone.

Brad and Mark were facing them as they skated backwards, gaining speed for the right second to turn and crowd the green-shirted puck carrier away from the Otter net and off the puck.

Thunderland's #2 lifted his stick to shoot. Mark moved. Thunderland countermoved with a drop pass to #11. He scored!

"Ohh—" the Oak River groan was lost in the boom of cheers from the Thunderland side of the rink. And so were the Otters' hopes for the first goal.

In the next shift, Coach Evans split Mark and Brad to send out Kurt and Brad.

"C'mon, Kurt. We've got to score!" Brad said. "We didn't get through that seven-mile snowdrift to fizzle out. Let's win it now!"

The face-off pattern formed. The puck dropped. Patterns changed. Brad circled back ready for a possible pass. A

Thunderland winger followed, leaving Kurt in the clear to intercept the puck.

He passed to Mike, who rushed for the slot before the green defense could close the gap. He shot!

Slap! Thunderland's goalie palmed the puck and dropped it to Thunderland's #11 who rushed past Mike, passed through Kurt, and drove full speed ahead. Before Brad could cross the ice to him, he took a long shot at the Oak River goal.

The puck smacked the crossbar, hit the back of Chug's helmet, and dropped behind the Otter goalie into the net!

A cheap goal! But it counted!

Two goals scored against the Otters, both when Brad was on the ice. The shame of a defenseman! He was working as hard as he could, but it wasn't enough. Brad had made two mistakes and Thunderland scored on both!

The shifts changed. Coach Evans's good nature had gone gruff. "Are you waiting till they pin you to the boards before you start checking?" he demanded of Kurt. "They've got your number. They'll pass right through you every time, *unless you start checking*. Defensemen are supposed to defend their net and each other." Art Evans threw up his hands then and turned back to the string of red players on the ice.

On the bench, Kurt mumbled to Brad, "Boy, I thought by the time we made it this far in tournament, I'd get over hating to check. I don't think it's fear of being hurt. It's just something inside me that rebels."

"So what else is new?" Brad added. "Every kid on the team has thought he was afraid to check at some time. Look at Coach."

Coach Evans paced up and down the box. He cringed at every check given to an Otter and ground his teeth at every check *not* given by an Otter.

"He's probably wondering why he ever—hey look, Kurt. We're controlling the puck. Look at Mark go!"

"Maybe they're not as good as they were the first game."

"Maybe we're not as scared!" Brad said.

Kurt grinned. "Maybe."

Fans shouted insults at the referee for not calling a Thunderland penalty.

Lines changed. Patterns formed and reformed. Fans on one side of the ice stood up when the fans on the other side sat down, as if the bleachers were built on an invisible teeter-totter. When play moved toward the Thunderland zone, Katie clanged her cowbell. When it swung toward the Oak River end, the Thunderland fans blew horns.

At rest shift, Coach was worrying again. "Why, Pete, why don't you shoot? This is a championship game. You're a centerman. Don't you want to win?"

Pete shrugged.

Coach threw up his arms in disgust. Then in a calm, but angry voice he said, "I don't know what's bugging you, kid. But if you skated like a professional, I still wouldn't have picked you for this team, if I'd known you didn't care!

"But you *are* on this team. You owe it to the team to play your position the very best you can. I didn't say play it better than anyone else on the team, I said the very best you can!"

Brad followed Pete's glance down the bench at gloved hands hanging onto upright sticks, shoulders sagging under soggy padding, and a couple of boys breathing heavily. Sweat dripped from under every red helmet.

Mark stretched for a long pass, but couldn't reach it before play was stopped. Coach Evans leaned over the boards and yelled, "Get it put together, boys!"

The puck dropped, but the whistle blew to end the first period. The scoreboard flashed 2-0 for Thunderland.

Coach Evans was waiting for his team when they reached the bench. "We've two periods to go and we're down by two goals. They think they have us! Whether they know it or not,

Thunderland will ease up now, then pour it on in the third period.

"So you can't do it in the third period. You've got to take them by surprise now! Just put it together!" He was begging now. "Four goals this period? I know you can do it. You've got the hockey talent to take this Thunderland team if *all* of you would just put it together. What's it going to take to get you to do that?"

Put it together. Put it together. Mom had said much the same to Brad. You can be right on the inside or right on the outside—but it takes the Lord to put it all together.

Thunderland won the drop, passed behind Kurt, and headed for open ice.

Flip zoomed in and hip-checked [19] #2 out of play. Pete picked up the puck, then reversed play with an across-ice pass to Brad.

Brad swept the ice as he lifted the puck into a hard shot. Right on! Wham! But it was deflected by the goalie's flashing butterfly drop.

Faster than Brad saw, Pete rebounded the puck into the net. It went in! The light went on! The sticks went up! The boys hugged and pounded each other shouting, "We scored! We scored!"

The Oak River fans cheered and cheered. The younger fans kept the cheers rolling, drowning out the announcer's official ruling on credit for the goal and assist. But the puck was in the right net, so who cared about anything else!

Slowly, over the next few minutes, the Oak River team jelled. Every pass they made connected with a teammate's stick. Every drive went through. Every check left them in the clear. The Otters could suddenly do no wrong.

Only Thunderland's unbelievably good goaltending kept the score in their favor, 2-1.

---

[19] *Hip check:* One player using his hip to slow down an opposing puck carrier. It is a legal check which takes strength and timing to perform well.

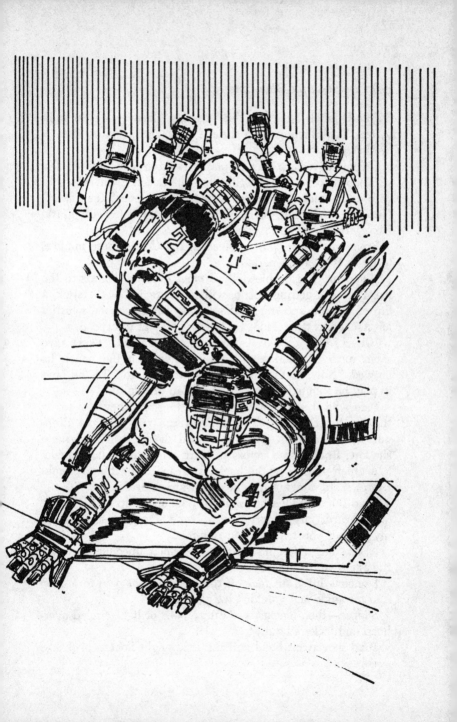

Dyn-O-mite! This was like tryouts all over again, only better. That feeling of a Friend that sticks closer than a brother.

Green-and-red patterns of play formed in loops and circles.

"Keep shooting, boys! Drill them in!" Coach Evans was wild with excitement. "No goalie is that good forever. Keep at it!" He alternated Brad, Kurt, Flip, Mike, and Pete with Mark, Don, Jerry, Sam, and Andy.

From the bench Brad glanced at the clock. Three minutes to go in the second period.

When the whistle blew, Brad went over the boards to the ice. Play was getting hectic, with an extra jab of the stick, a flip of the fist, and dig of the skates. Time between whistles lengthened as the refs let both teams play at top speed.

"Check, boy, check!" Coach Evans bellowed. "Don't give them room to wind up." To the players on the bench he crowed, "Now, that's hockey! Look at them go!" To the boys in play he shouted, "You can do it! You can do it!"

Pete won the face-off and passed to Flip. They moved up the ice together. Big Thunderland #8 rushed. Pete drop-passed to Brad. Cut off from a good shot by a Thunderland shadow, Brad passed across to Kurt, who passed back again.

A green player saw the backpass, reached for it, and caught Brad's skate, flinging him face forward onto the ice.

Brad felt a sudden hot shaft of pain shoot up his right leg.

He heard Gary's angry threats boom across the ice: "That's my brother you tripped, you dummie!"

A moaning filled his ears that seemed unconnected with the agony in his leg.

Someone lifted his face off the ice. A jolt of pain tore deep into his ankle and wouldn't let go.

Silence—then blackness— Fuzzy balls of light circled overhead and flickered out.

Brad moved his head and the fuzzy light floated back like

dandelion fluff on a summer breeze. Then he saw steel beams outlined overhead, and Kurt, red-faced and scowling. Pete was holding a red helmet with #4 on it.

That's mine, Brad thought. *What's he doing with my helmet?* But he couldn't complete the idea for the pain took over again. He couldn't fit the pieces together. He knew he was in an arena, but where was the clush-shush of skates, the clash of bodies, the shouts and whistles? He'd never been in an arena this silent before.

He heard coach ask, "OK, now?"

"Sure," Brad tried to rise, but another hot shaft of pain pulled him down. "Except for my leg."

Art Evans and Joe LaBlanc each took an arm and pulled Brad up. He hung between them, his left skate on the ice, his right knee bent. The pain pulled him back into blackness.

At the gate Brad roused enough to know that a big skier reached out and lifted him up—all 128 pounds of him. The skier carried Brad through the crowd, cradled in his powerful arms.

Brad opened his eyes to see his Aunt Kate's face, but she seemed to float away from him before he could speak to her. Somehow he seemed 10 feet off the ground, suspended in pain.

He saw the trophy case, a bright glitter in the gray fog of his mind. Then he slid downward into painless darkness.

14

 Money in a Cup

It seemed like years later that the blackness around Brad parted again. He couldn't be sure for his thoughts came like foggy pictures edged in sunlight.

He remembered the backpass coming straight from Kurt's stick to his own, just inside the blue line. It was a perfect shot! Slam!

Then the pictures skipped to a circle of faces like people peering over the rim of a deep dark well. Only Brad was in the darkness looking up at them. Mark, Jerry, and Pete were looking down.

Then the dream did a flip-flop to a close-up of a skier, so close Brad saw the dark shadow of whiskers on his clean-shaven square jaw bracketed by dark sideburns.

Then an out-of-focus picture of Aunt Kate's face at Brad's eye level. And the trophy case with old, tarnished loving cups on the top shelves.

Then Brad heard voices that sounded like a whole dressing room full of players. He could see Mark, Jerry, Kurt, Pete, and Coach Evans. They were smiling, their shining faces sweaty with joy!

"Hey guys, I had a dream," Brad heard himself saying. "I dreamed we won the Grand Championship!"

"That was no dream," Mark said. "We did! We did! I just told you that! But you keep wanting to go back to sleep. Brad, *WE WON THE GRAND CHAMPIONSHIP!*"

Brad stared wide-eyed, trying to ward off the fuzziness in his mind. The whole hockey team seemed to phase in and out of this wonderful dream he was having. Only it wasn't a dream! And it wasn't wonderful. He was lying in the hospital with a broken leg!

Mark was standing beside his bed hanging onto a great golden loving cup.

"Hey, Turkey! Did you hear me this time?" Mark added. "We beat the unbeatables! 6-4."

"And we did it all for you!" Someone clowned.

A nurse came in and threatened: "Quiet or you'll have to leave."

So Mark acted as spokesman and explained. "Your mom told us you were still drowsy from getting your leg set, but we just had to come and show you." He held the huge trophy for Brad to see. *Georgian Valley Apple Growers Association. Bantam, Grand Champions.*

"After you were hit, 'Boomer' here came on like a bull-dozer." Mark and the others pounded Kurt on the back. "He checked everything that touched the puck."

"And Pete here got three goals in the third period!" Coach Evans crowed. "I told you so, Pete. I knew you had it in you!"

Brad could hardly believe his ears. "Wow! You guys do better without me!"

"We did it all backwards," Jerry said. "We didn't get the first goal, we didn't take the lead in the second period, and we didn't win on endurance. But we won anyway!"

Coach Evans broke in, "We won because we just plain

wanted to get out there and put it all together!" He grinned at Brad. "You get some rest now. I hope that ankle heals fast." He and Jerry and Mark turned to go, leaving just Kurt and Pete.

"You know, Brad," Kurt said as he looked at Brad's lumpy form under the sheet, "Gary told me one day that all that superreligious talk about Jesus doesn't change how a guy feels." He spoke softly with that sidewise smile as he added, "But I have an idea that all the bad breaks don't change how a guy feels about life either—at least not when he has it all straight inside like you do."

Brad smiled, surprised at his friend's new understanding. "I guess prayer helps a guy see things straight," he answered.

"Dad's waiting for me," Kurt said. "He got in from Montreal in time to see the last half of the last period, but I didn't know it till the game was over." Then Kurt was gone.

Only Pete remained in the hospital room.

"Pete, I had a beautiful dream sometime when I was unconscious. I dreamed Pete Paquette carried me to the hospital from the rink. Imagine that! An NHL super centerman here at our Georgian Valley Tournament."

Brad chuckled over it. "He said, 'the way you can tell a real pro is by the way he handles himself when he's hurt.' He said I'd make it. Wow! Wasn't that a fantastic dream?"

"That was no dream," Pete said. "It really happened. He didn't *carry* you here, but he did carry you to his car and *drove* you here."

Brad couldn't believe it. "What would Pete Paquette be doing here—in Beaver Bridge?" He tried to remember the NHL schedule of games. "He plays in the Maple Leaf Gardens in Toronto tonight."

Pete nodded. "Toronto is 100 miles from here. About an hour and a half, the way he drives that red Corvette of his."

"It was that skier who carried me here," Brad said.

"And that skier is Pete Paquette." Pete pulled back the hospital sheet. "See."

There, at the top of Brad's white cast, scrawled in a black marker pen, was the autograph of Pete Paquette.

"It wasn't a dream? But how? Why?"

Pete grinned. "He's my dad." Then he went on to explain, "Remember the skier who helped us the day Mom and I were stuck?" Pete continued. "That was Dad. Mom was so mad about that, that's why I missed that practice. She was still chewing him out at 10 o'clock that night. She was afraid he'd blow our cover."

"Dyn-O-mite! Pete Paquette for a dad! But why did you keep it a secret? Wow! I'd give anything just to have any decent dad. And you have Pete Paquette. Wow! What a super dad!"

"You say that because you've never had a hockey star for a father," Pete said. "Almost every kid in Canada hopes to play with the big league hockey leagues someday. Me too! But every goof I make is 100 times worse than any you guys make—I'm supposed to know better because I'm Big Pete's son.

"Every good move I make is suddenly zilch—because I'm Big Pete's son, and that's expected of me!"

This reminded Brad of the way he'd felt the night he brought home the rink helmet, shouting that he'd made the team. Pete's problem was Brad's problem, and every kid's problem: To be himself!

"I can feel how it was, Pete. But imagine? Big Pete Paquette and I can't even tell!"

Pete shrugged. "Maybe it's not so important now. You see, Brad, a doctor in my last school told Mom that the superstar performance Mom and Dad expected wasn't good for me. He told Mom I was a school kid, not a highly paid hockey star, and shouldn't be expected to act like one.

"So Mom didn't skate with the Icecapades this year. We moved to Oak River where nobody knew me as the son of Pete Paquette or the son of Julia Peters, an Ice Capades skating star. So—"

"Dyn-O-mite!" was all Brad could say.

"Mom and Dad agreed to let me live for this one year like any other kid who wants to play hockey. And it's been great! Before, it was awful! When word got around an arena that Pete Paquette was there, the kids were suddenly playing to empty bleachers. The fans were getting Big Pete's autograph for themselves or their cousins or their grandchildren."

Even after Pete's explanation, Brad found it hard to believe. He looked at the autograph again. "Wow." It sent a tingle of excitement all through him. The skin under the drying cast burned. But the thought of Big Pete Paquette actually saying, "You can tell a real pro by the way he handles himself when he's hurt," was like medicine.

Pete grinned at Brad. "Coach Evans has been after me to play better. But with so much professional coaching from Dad and Mom too, I guess I just hated all coaching. Today Coach told me he wouldn't have me on his team even if I skated like an NHL pro if I didn't care.

"Well, when you got hurt, Brad, I suddenly started caring. I played hockey for my team, not for Pete Paquette or Julia Peters. And how I loved it!"

"Dyn-O-mite!" Brad exclaimed. "I knew you had the best equipment and more hockey shirts than I'd ever seen in my life. But Pete Peters is—"

"Pete Peters Paquette, centerman with the Oak River Otters who just won the Georgian Valley championship," Pete finished, laughing.

After Pete left, Brad slept. He roused when he heard his mother's footsteps. He tried to turn, forgetting about the 10-pound cast.

"Mom? Are we really the grand champions? Was the game really that great?" Brad still needed reassurance that it wasn't all a dream.

"You are and it was." His mom laughed. "Dyn-O-mite! The whole place was charged with excitement. Even Gary got carried away. He nearly fell over the boards, yelling down at the Thunderland player who took you out of play. He kept screaming, 'That's my brother you tripped, you dummie!'

"And something else. Your brother is just as responsible for the Otters winning the championship as anyone on the team. I'm so proud of him."

"What do you mean?" Brad demanded, his eyes wide and mouth open.

"That TV newscaster, Matt, told me that Gary overheard you fellows groaning about Mark and the sweaters not arriving on time. When he realized what was wrong, he grabbed Matt and got the officials' permission to let Matt interview Thunderland in their dressing room—to stall for time. Matt just finished interviewing them when you fellows burst onto the ice."

"Wow, what do you know!" Brad was awed. "That brother of mine has quite a head on him! By the way, Mom, where is he now?"

"With Aunt Kate. She was late and just got there in time to see you carried out." Mom was looking at the trophy the fellows had left, running her finger around the cup's rolled edge. "The newsman said he'd drop over and get a shot of you in case nothing like a murder or a rebellion turns up, and he needs news footage over the weekend."

Brad stared at the trophy, thinking there was something he should remember to tell his mother, but it seemed to be lost in his dreamworld pictures of foggy light and dandelion fluff. Finally it came to him. "Mom, I dreamed I saw the stolen money," he said slowly.

"Hey, that's the kind of dream a newsman needs," Matt Bolton said as he strode into the room.

Brad struggled to bring his dream back, but all he got were jigsaw pieces, that didn't fit.

When he first woke from having his leg set, he'd thought winning the championship was a dream. But it wasn't. They had won. There was the trophy to prove it.

Even the wild dream of Pete Paquette bringing him to the hospital had turned out to be real. He had the cast and his autograph on it.

And Aunt Kate had been at the arena. Mom said so.

And the money?

It was Robby Westbrook who'd called Gary the trophy watcher. Maybe it was really Gary the *money watcher?*

Suddenly all Brad's fears and suspicions were back. He shook his head as if to shake the pieces of the jigsaw puzzle into place, to form a picture more to his liking.

Brad looked from his mother to Matt, as they talked about Gary buying time for the team. They were laughing.

"Mom, where is Gary?" Brad asked again.

"He's coming with Aunt Kate. We had our lunch at the hospital cafeteria," his mother said.

"Gary in a cafeteria? Voluntarily? I thought he'd rather starve first!" Brad was amazed.

Matt laughed. "Don't be surprised at anything that brother of yours does, now that he's started!"

That's why Brad worried about Gary and the money.

"Hey, what about that money, kid? A poor roving reporter needs every break he can get in these be-nice-to-your-neighbor communities around here. When they say crime doesn't pay, they mean the criminal, but it does pay the newsman's bills."

"I think I dreamed I saw a bundle of bills inside a loving cup but I can't figure it out."

"But that trophy case is kept locked all the time," Matt said, puzzled.

"It must have been opened today to get this trophy out," Brad said.

"And it was open when the cash table was dumped," Mom said. "Remember, Brad? Mr. Jaleski had the cup in one hand while he directed the crowd with the other."

"Hey, that's right. Thunderland, as last year's champion, was returning the trophy to the host rink for this year's competition. Wow!" Brad felt a bubble rising in his spirit. For Gary was sitting on his crutches on the floor when the trophy case was opened and left unattended. Then the thief must have been someone at the edge of the crowd, someone who got through the crowd before Gary did, for Gary was on the bottom of the pile. A hockey player? Or . . . Robby Westbrook?

Something popped into Brad's head, "every idle word that man shall speak—give account—" (Matthew 12:36). But before he could voice any of his thoughts, Aunt Kate came in with Gary right behind her.

"Hey, Gary, did you see anything odd about the trophy case?" Brad asked even before greetings could be exchanged.

Gary's head snapped up from his crutch slouch. "Why? What should I see besides trophies?"

"That's what I'm trying to figure out," Brad said.

"You and me both," Gary grumbled. "I've been trying to figure it out for four games. There's something about that trophy case that flaps that Westbrook kid. Something I should see and don't. Or else I'm seeing it and don't know it yet."

"Were you there when Jake Jaleski took our trophy out?" Brad asked.

"Yeah," Gary nodded.

"Was Robby Westbrook there?"

"Yeah, and was he nervous about something!"

Brad told him then of the dream that must not be a dream. "That's it!" Gary shouted. "The dust on the top shelf where the old trophies are kept was disturbed. One cup had been moved because there was a crescent-shaped area that wasn't dusty."

"Want to solve a crime?" Matt asked Gary. Gary was out the door just three crutch steps behind the newsman.

Brad lay back grinning a broad, brotherly grin.

When the local sports news came on that night, he was still grinning: "Oak River, the unknowns in the Georgian Valley Tournament, worked their way down the losing side and dumped the unbeaten Thunderland Bantam team.

"It started out as a so-so hockey game but turned thunderous when a battle at the blue line sent one Oak River boy to the hospital with a fractured lower tibia. That accident turned a loose-knit bunch of boys into a tough hockey team. Congratulations to the Oak River All-star Bantams!"

The next day, after Brad was home, he heard the newscast about the money: "There was more than glory in ye old loving cups at the Georgian Valley Apple Grower's Tournament this year. The stolen money was not really stolen, just misplaced. It wasn't taken from the Beaver Bridge Arena, just hidden in a trophy. But then rink manager, Jake Jaleski, locked the case. It wasn't until the case was broken into—"

"Jake Jaleski and his son Steve were cleaning up after the games when Matt and I got there yesterday," Gary interrupted to explain. "And Robby was there too—in the dark by the trophy case. Matt mentioned the trophy case and Robby must have heard. He dropped a screwdriver and ran. He had one hinge off and one more to go."

Brad watched his brother talking excitedly and felt the bubble of joy all over again. "Jake said he wouldn't press charges, but he was going to suggest to Robby's dad that the kid should do 50 laps a day around the arena, until he learned to skate without cheating. He's a firm believer in working the cheating out of kids."

Brad reached for his crutches and stood up, settling his weight onto the wooden supports. He stood facing his brother, leaning in the same position on his metal crutches.

"Oh no!" Aunt Kate laughed. "What's worse than one boy on crutches, Ruth? Two!"

Mom was smiling. "It's what's better than one boy on crutches? Two!"

The boys stared at each other. It wasn't funny, but they both burst out laughing.

Gary stopped suddenly. "Just wait until this championship fever wears off, big hockey player, and you realize you won't be skating for the rest of the hockey season or speed-skating in the winter carnival or playing for the school hockey team either. Just wait until you find out everything it rips off."

Brad was still smiling. "I'll make it with my Friend's help."

"Hmph! You'll be a bear with a sore leg when—"

"Gary, you forget that your mom is a pro at looking after bears with sore legs," Aunt Kate said.

"There'll be tears," Gary warned, "because you'll hurt inside—where the doctor can't put a cast on."

"But in there . . . my Friend cares and knows what I need," Brad insisted.

"That I believe," Aunt Kate said. "Knowing Brad, as soon as he gets a walking cast on, he'll invent a new game. Instead of broomball, it'll be crutch ball."

A week later, when Aunt Kate came out again, she handed Brad a model airplane kit similar to those she'd brought Gary when he was first home from the hospital in a wheelchair. "You'll have to help your brother, Gary. He's never sat still long enough to develop a skill for this kind of thing."

"Oh, brother!" was all Gary said, but it wasn't an unbrotherly sound. "If those crummy Otters can get it all together like that and play their way out of a losing situation, then so can I."

Brad looked up startled.

"Not in hockey, you dummie," Gary said. "In life!"

After supper, when Mom poured coffee for her and Aunt Kate to take to the living room, Gary picked up his crutches and said, "C'mon, Brad. Let's get at it. You don't do dishes with your lower tibia, you know!"